BURN FOR YOU

Into The Fire Series

J.H. CROIX

J.H. CROIX

 Created with Vellum

"The very essence of romance is uncertainty." -Oscar Wilde

Sign up for my newsletter for information on new releases & get a FREE copy of one of my books!

http://jhcroixauthor.com/subscribe/

Follow me!
jhcroix@jhcroix.com
https://amazon.com/author/jhcroix
https://www.bookbub.com/authors/j-h-croix
https://www.facebook.com/jhcroix
https://www.instagram.com/jhcroix/

BURN FOR YOU

A date auction gone wrong. Or so *very* right.

Holly

The whole mess started with a fundraiser. You know, those date auctions?

It was for a good cause. I swear. But then Nate Fox won the date with me. Nate who drives me *insane*.

He's my brother's best friend, and oh-so-inconveniently sexy as h*ll. He also spent some serious cash for that date. With *me*.

It's a disaster in the making, and I'll do whatever I must to avoid it. Small problem though. Nate's insisting I make good on it.

A date with him is bad enough. Even worse, I want him. Fiercely.

Nate

The moment I look up and see Holly Blake walk out on that

stage, I'm determined to make my longest running fantasy come true.

I'll have my second chance with Holly. Even if I have to pay for it. She's smart, sassy, and so d*mn gorgeous.

Then, I find out she has a secret. A secret that only makes me want her even more.

*This is a full-length, standalone romance with a guaranteed HEA.

Chapter One

HOLLY

PSA: Dating sucks.

I was staring down thirty—two years away was too close, as far as I was concerned—and not really looking forward to it. I was additionally annoyed with myself for actually caring about the fact that I was turning thirty. I didn't like to think of myself as one of those women who obsessed over her age.

Apparently, I was. Or at least, lately. You see, all my friends kept falling in love. I was happy for them. I truly was. Cross my heart and hope to die, I was not exaggerating about that. But, well, I was starting to feel left behind. My friends were even having babies. Babies! And I'd yet to even find a man, or woman, or mythical creature, much less procreate. I refused to let myself become one of those bitter spinsters.

That said, trying to date in a small town in Alaska had its challenges. I loved Willow Brook. It was my hometown, and I'd never been the kind of person who needed to leave to remember how much I loved it. Not that there was anything wrong with that. I had tons of friends and family, and I couldn't imagine living anywhere else. But *you* try meeting someone new when most everybody in town has known you since you were in preschool.

Correction: since you were a baby. But I didn't remember the baby stuff, so I sure as hell hoped nobody else did either. All of this led to a point. Or rather, a place and an event, and the reason why I was there.

I adjusted my rather tight nurse costume. In real life, nurses like myself wore scrubs and practical shoes. *Not* so sexy. In fact, comfort and getting bloodstains out was more important than looking good. The whole nurse costume thing was considered sexy, which had always cracked me up. Trust me, when you dealt with bodily fluids and seeing people often at their most vulnerable, there was very little about it that was sexy.

I loved my job, though. I was one of the head Emergency Department nurses at Willow Brook Hospital. I was living in my favorite place, doing work I loved. Even helping random tourists get fishing hooks out of God knows where on their body felt worthy.

Great job, great town, great friends and family ... and a whopping *zero* dating prospects for me. That was what probably landed me in my current situation. Somehow, I'd gotten roped into offering myself up for a date for a hospital fundraiser in Anchorage. The only reason I agreed was because I thought it'd be funny as hell. No one here would know me, and maybe, just maybe, I'd actually meet someone.

With Anchorage close to an hour away from Willow Brook, the possibility of meeting someone new shimmered on the invisible horizon. Plus, Anchorage was an actual city.

Standing backstage, I was a little nervous. Not only was this an auctioned date function, but it was for Halloween. Hence, why I was wearing a costume. For the first time since I'd become a nurse, I was dressed sexy.

Damn, even I had to admit I looked good. My rather annoyingly generous breasts were squished into this nurse costume, practically spilling out the top.

I'm sure you can imagine it. One of those tight little white numbers, with buttons up the middle of the fitted blouse, like no nurse would ever wear. It was snug at my waist and then flared out into a short little skirt, which barely covered my too-big ass. I was feeling slightly self-conscious.

My old friend from nursing school, Megan, had not informed me just how suggestive these costumes would be. I felt like a stripper.

"Oh my God, you look great," Megan said, as if she'd managed to read my mind from the other room. She closed the door behind her as she stepped into the small dressing room behind the stage.

The fundraiser was being held in a large auditorium in downtown Anchorage, frequently used for local performances and the like.

"You neglected to mention how small this was," I said, pinning her with a glare.

Megan shrugged. "You look totally hot. I'm doing it too. See?" she said, gesturing up and down her body.

"How come you got the fisher-girl outfit?" I asked as I scanned her costume.

She was wearing bright red fishing waders and a silky fitted tank top. Don't get me wrong, it was revealing, but it wasn't nearly as skimpy as what I was wearing.

Megan grinned. "You're way sexier than me. I've got no ass to speak of, and you've got curves for days. I'm not back here to debate your costume, though. You're up in about ten minutes. I'm so glad you agreed to do this! I think you're gonna make the most money for us tonight."

"You sound like my pimp. I'm honored."

Megan was unmoved. She simply winked. "I'm happy to be your pimp. If you want me to find you a man, I'm all over that shit. Come on," she said, gesturing for me to follow her. "I wish we'd saved you for last because you're definitely the hottest."

Seeing as most of my best friends were married, engaged, pregnant, or on the way to being pregnant, Megan was one of the few friends I confided in lately about my man troubles. Like me, she was still single. Unlike me, she wasn't really looking.

As I walked through the hallway, which was crowded with people prepping for the fundraiser, my belly started to coil with anxiety, and I felt flushed with heat. I suddenly realized this was an absolutely insane thing to do. The idea of it had seemed amusing and cute from a distance. But now, with my boobs nearly bursting out of my nurse costume, my butt just barely covered, and my bright red high heels, I was feeling just a teensy bit self-conscious.

Conveniently, there was alcohol backstage. I stopped by the bar, which was nothing more than a plastic table set up in the back, and smiled at the man behind it. He flashed a grin.

"What can I get you, dear? You look gorgeous, and you're going to make us a ton of money."

Inhaling a gulp of air, I let it out with a sigh. This man wasn't looking at me like he was going to eat me up, so I felt okay. "I'll take two shots of tequila," I replied.

The man's smile softened. "I would reconsider and stick with one. I'm Ethan, by the way."

"I'm Holly," I returned. "I still think I need two shots. How did you get roped into being a backstage bartender?"

Ethan chuckled as he poured me a single shot—generous, but just one. "My partner, Jack, and I own the Midnight Sun Arts galleries here in Anchorage and a few other locations. We help run a number of fundraisers. This is a good one. Absolutely all of the money raised goes into a funding pool to cover uninsured patients at hospitals all over Alaska. That's why we do so much on this one. Everybody you see here is volunteering."

He handed me my first shot. "Let's start with one."

"Oh no," I said with a shake of my head. "I've got ten minutes. I need two."

I gulped down the first shot, the burn of it quick and satisfying. Ethan eyed me and poured another shot. After my second one, I felt like I might have enough liquid courage to get me through this madness.

Ethan chatted with me while I waited, his easygoing manner calming me. Within a few minutes, Megan was ushering me out onto the stage.

As soon as I stepped out, I relaxed. It helped that I was just tipsy enough not to give much of a damn. I did my thing as instructed, walking across the stage and spinning in a circle, almost losing my balance in the process. Thank God I couldn't really see the crowd with the bright lights, seeing as my wobble got a laugh.

The auctioneer handled the bidding. Before I knew it, someone had "bought" a date with me for five thousand dollars. You heard me right—five thousand dollars.

Dizzy and more than a little buzzed by the time I got off the stage, I walked backstage. Megan flashed me a wink and a giant thumbs-up. Ethan, who I decided was my new best friend, shepherded me to a room where I was allegedly going to meet whoever the hell purchased a charity date with me. He paused outside the door, offering a warm smile.

"Well, dear, this man definitely wanted you. You just beat the last highest bid we've ever had by two grand."

All I could manage was a nod. With the tequila hitting me harder, I didn't care anymore. Crazy as this had been, at least I raised five thousand dollars for the hospital program. Ethan ushered me into a small room in the back where there was a table with a few bottles of alcohol and two chairs. They seemed to think if they scattered alcohol everywhere, people would be stupid enough to do this. I supposed I was the example of why they were right. I didn't really know how this thing worked. Apparently, my date could either have the date with me tonight, or later. I was thinking tonight was not the best plan, considering my tipsy state.

Within a minute, the door opened again. The moment my eyes landed on the man in question, my mouth fell open. Instead of my date, Nate Fox stepped into the room—all six-feet-four-inches of him with shaggy brown curls, flashing brown eyes, and a body made for sin.

Nate Fox was also my twin brother's best friend and the younger brother of my best friend's husband.

Even worse, I totally had a thing for Nate. In fact, one drunken night, about a year ago, we'd come dangerously close to fucking each other in the coat closet at a friend's party.

My twin brother had conveniently interrupted us. Alex was so oblivious, he didn't even pick up on the cues. Or perhaps he did and preferred to ignore my hastily yanked together blouse, which I later discovered had been buttoned lopsided.

Despite crossing paths almost weekly, Nate and I managed to keep every interaction entirely superficial since then. Let me tell you, that was no easy feat in our small social circles. Nate had it all but written on his forehead he wanted nothing more to do with me, so I figured too much alcohol had gotten to him. I needed to get my head out of my ass and stop wishing he wanted more.

The moment the door clicked shut behind him, I was just drunk enough to be pissed off. "What the hell are you doing here?" I demanded.

He crossed the room, stopping maybe a foot away from me.

"What the hell are *you* doing here?" he countered in return, his eyes narrowing and his words coming out sharp.

"What does it look like I'm doing? I'm doing this fundraiser for the hospital. Get the hell out of here." I waved my hand. "Someone just paid five thousand bucks for a date with me, and I'm not gonna screw it up by having you here when they show up," I muttered, my speech slurring a little.

Nate stared at me for a beat, his eyes taking on a wicked gleam before his mouth kicked up at the corner. "Oh, you don't need to worry about that. I'm the one who bought a date with you."

My body was on fire, heat flashing through it in a rush and my belly spinning in flips at the raw desire in his eyes. Nate drove me crazy. He'd been Alex's best friend for as long as I could remember. If you'd told me I'd have thought he would be sexy when I was about ten, I'd have laughed until I peed my pants.

Everything had felt normal until sometime over a year ago. As if tectonic plates shifted in the earth, I looked at Nate one day and suddenly noticed he was obscenely handsome. Making out with him that night was the biggest mistake I'd ever made. Desire had shifted from a loose idea into something concrete, very real, and very intense.

Nate annoyed me. He always told me what to do, just like my brother. The last thing I needed to do was to be attracted to him. Unfortunately, my body wasn't getting the memo. Just now, my panties were already giving up the fight.

"Oh, I don't think so. I'll do it all over again if I have to. I'm sure you can get a refund."

Meanwhile, my nipples stood at attention and my channel clenched, vividly remembering the feel of his fingers buried inside me.

Chapter Two

NATE

Holly Blake stood defiantly before me, testing every ounce of my restraint. But then, she'd been testing me for *years*. With her thick blonde hair loose around her shoulders and her curvy body poured into her outfit, I could hardly think.

At the moment, I couldn't even remember how I ended up at this fucking fundraiser. Not that I had anything against fundraisers. My memory shifted into gear, kicking through the haze of raw lust Holly's mere presence had created. My buddy had roped me into going because he'd been dragged into helping out. I was there for moral support only. The last thing I expected was to bid on a date with someone. But the second I'd seen Holly on the stage, there was no fucking way I was letting someone else win a date with her.

I'd been speechless—not something that happened often, by the way—when Holly pranced out on the stage in the sexiest excuse for a nursing costume I'd ever seen. Sweet Jesus. If I didn't screw her right now against the wall, I deserved a fucking medal.

Her breasts were spilling out of the tight blouse, and I was pretty sure I could see her panties if she bent over even a little. I idly wondered if they were red to match her bright red high heels.

I took a deep breath, shackling the need galloping through my body. What the hell had she just said? Oh yeah.

"I got the winning bid, and I don't want a refund," I replied.

Her brown eyes widened and then narrowed. I was pretty sure she was a little drunk. Holly had never been one to hold back, but right now, she was a little freer than usual, let's just say.

"Why?" she demanded.

"Jesus, Holly. You're fucking parading around out there half-naked. Trust me, I saw your options. I'm your best bet. The guy who I outbid was pushing seventy. Not that there's anything wrong with being old, but I don't think he's your type. What the hell are you doing here anyway?"

I knew I sounded pissed off. I also knew I had no right to feel that way, but it didn't change anything.

Holly spun around, flinging a hand up in the air and giving me the finger as she walked to the far side of the room. Not that the room was too large. She turned back to me, crossing her arms and setting her feet apart.

"What the hell are you doing here? Like I said before, I'm here to raise money for charity. That's why. And I sure as hell don't need you fucking everything up. I might actually get to meet somebody here. But now you're here, so I'm stuck with you."

My head was spinning as I tried to catch up to what she was implying. "What the fuck do you mean? You might meet someone?"

Holly sighed, letting her arms fall and resting a hand on her hip. Holly was all kinds of tempting. Her blonde hair was most often pulled up in a slapdash ponytail, and she was usually wearing scrubs. Even when she made zero effort to look good, she was sexy as sin. Dressed like this?

I was so screwed.

"I need another shot," she muttered, turning around and walking to a table in the corner where, lo and behold, there were a few bottles of alcohol. She proceeded to pour a shot of tequila and knock it back inside of a few seconds.

"It's not like my dating prospects are any good in Willow Brook," she mumbled as she turned back to face me. "I figured I'd raise a little money for this hospital thing and maybe I might actually meet someone. Not you. I didn't need to meet you."

For the second time tonight, I was speechless.

Fuck it.

I strode to her, reaching for her hands and tugging her against me.

"What do you think you're doing?" she murmured as her body bumped against mine.

"You don't need to meet anybody," I said flatly.

Holly's breath hissed through her teeth. When she gulped in air, her breasts pressed against my chest. It was then I realized my miscalculation. Because I couldn't be near Holly and not want her. Fiercely.

Having her this close meant there was no way for her to miss the fact that I was rock hard and ready. Her eyes narrowed again, and she jabbed her finger in my chest.

"You don't get to say whether or not I need to meet anybody. You're not my keeper, so don't fucking act like it."

"No. But I want you, and I know you want me. So, let's stop dancing around and do something about it."

Her mouth dropped open, her cheeks flushing bright pink and sending another shot of blood straight to my swollen cock.

"You don't know that I want you," she announced, with another jab of her finger against my chest. "You've been ignoring me anyway."

"You mean to tell me you forgot about that kiss last year," I murmured, sliding my palm down the back of her spine to cup her bottom, palming it as I rocked into her slightly.

She rolled her eyes. "I'm not trying to tell you I forgot about it. But you couldn't run away fast enough. I'm not an idiot. I'm not just gonna be another chick you have a little fun with. I'm almost thirty, and I need something real, not you and your bullshit."

"Oh sweetheart, this isn't bullshit."

I finally gave into the need I'd been holding at bay for too damn long. I fit my mouth over hers, growling at the snap of electricity the moment our lips collided.

That kiss we had a year ago? It was as if we picked up right where we left off. My body knew exactly what it wanted. I swept my tongue into the warm sweetness of her mouth, savoring the low moan coming from her throat and the way she flexed into me.

Just when I forgot where we were and what the hell I was doing, there was a sharp knock at the door. Holly broke away from me, stumbling back. The door swung open, and one of the guys who'd been helping with the tickets at the main door when I first got here stepped into the room.

"How we doing here?" he asked with a smile as his gaze swept over us.

We'd kissed maybe for a minute, yet Holly's lips were swollen, her skin was flushed, and my arousal was likely quite evident to anyone who paid attention.

Holly's gaze swung to the man. "Ethan, I'm so glad you're here. We have a problem."

What the fuck is she doing?

Holly approached Ethan, looping her arm through his, and then pointing to me. "He's not the right date. I grew up with him, so this won't work," she said flatly.

Ethan's lips tightened as he fought a smile, his gaze flicking to me and then back to her. "Sweetheart, it doesn't quite work that way. He paid for a date with you. Short of things like violence or safety, either you're going on a date with him, or we refund him his money. Unless he agrees to forfeit the date," he said carefully.

"Can't his money pay for somebody else?" Holly asked, undeterred.

I was trying to keep a level head, but now I was pissed. "No," I said sharply. "You don't have to go on a date with me. But I'm not paying for someone else. Before you go making up something ridiculous"—I paused, looking at Ethan—"her twin brother is my best friend. We've known each other forever. There's nothing nefarious here."

Ethan was quiet, his gaze bouncing between us. "Well, then I'm sure you two can figure this out. Holly," he said, gently uncurling her hand from his arm, "if you would like us to refund his money, please let me know. Otherwise, I'll leave you two alone for now."

As soon as the door shut behind him, I strode to her. Conveniently, she was standing beside the wall. I placed my hands on the wall beside her and pinned my gaze on hers.

"You're a coward," I said flatly.

"I'm not a coward!"

"I say you are. Plus, maybe you're not giving me enough credit."

"I'm sorry?"

"You're right. After that kiss last year, I kept my distance. Because I didn't want to be stupid. You're my best friend's sister, so there's that hurdle. I want you more than I've ever wanted anyone. I didn't know if I was ready to do anything about it. Now I am. The ball is in your court."

I held still for a moment before trailing my fingers down her shoulder, teasing over her tight little nipple, and then over the soft curve of her hip. Stopping there took all of my restraint, but I managed it.

I stepped back. "You owe me a date. Tell me now if you're backing out. I'll leave you alone if you are, but don't play games with me."

Holly's breath came in shallow little pants. She shifted

her legs, and I heard her rubbing her thighs together, just barely. I hadn't forgotten how wet she'd been last year when I lost my damn mind and almost fucked her at a party.

She stared at me, lifting her chin slightly. "I'm not backing out. When and where?"

"Your call. But not tonight. Let me make one thing clear, though. It will be a real date. You don't get to say, let's grab drinks at Wildlands, or coffee at Firehouse Café. Hell no. Dinner and a hotel. I did pay five thousand dollars, after all."

"I'm not your whore," she retorted.

I closed the distance between us again, leaning forward and catching her lips in another kiss. Kissing her was like playing with dynamite. Clinging to my control, I drew away.

"No, you are absolutely not. You want this as much as I do."

Chapter Three

HOLLY

Leaning across the desk in the nursing station, I snagged my cold cup of coffee. It was going on midnight, usually a quiet time at Willow Brook Hospital in the Emergency Department. I took a gulp of my coffee, spinning around when I heard my name. As luck would have it, somehow between taking a sip and moving at the same time, I spilled the remainder of the coffee all over the front of my scrubs.

And looked right into the eyes of Nate Fox.

Great, just great.

Nate's lips curled at the corners in a slow grin, promptly sending butterflies into flight in my belly and a flush straight to my cheeks.

"Well, hello, Holly," he said slowly, his eyes flicking down to the coffee, spilled all over my breasts, of course.

"Fuck," I muttered. Turning, my eyes landed on a box of tissue on the corner of the desk. I grabbed a handful, dabbing at the coffee, rather pointlessly, and tossed them in the trash.

"That helped," Nate said, his lips twitching.

Mustering my composure, I glanced up with a resigned sigh. "Hey, Nate. What can I do for you? You don't look injured."

He lifted his wrist, and then I noticed the swelling.

"I'm not sure if I broke it, or sprained it," he said matter-of-factly.

"Oh, okay, let's get you into a room so we can take a look. Follow me," I said, setting my coffee down and hurrying out from behind the counter of the nurse's station.

I was concerned Nate was injured, but also quite relieved to have something to focus on. My body practically caught on fire every time I thought about the last time I'd seen him. Which I did a lot. *A lot*, a lot.

If Nate was in pain, it didn't particularly show. But he was the kind of man who took pain in stride. He was also the kind of man who drove me crazy. I didn't like to contemplate just how thoroughly Nate had hijacked my brain and body. Just now though, I was all business.

He was pure man and way too handsome for his own good. With his dark brown hair and matching eyes, and a body made for drooling, he had plenty of women swooning over him. He was also a wilderness pilot, flying all over the skies in Alaska, via helicopter or plane, to ferry wilderness adventurers, deliver supplies, and to provide support to hotshot firefighters whenever and wherever needed. He was all about risk and adventure, and he held the key to getting under my skin. He drove me completely insane, and our last little interlude had nearly pushed me over the edge.

Stuffing those thoughts to the furthest corner of my mind, I walked down the hall with him at my side, acutely aware of his presence. He was potent, exuding a teasing sensuality that made my body hum. I forced my attention to the moment. Right now, he was here late at night because he had injured his hand. As the head nurse on duty for the ER, I needed to do my damn job.

I reminded myself sternly that I needed to be professional and not let my pesky thoughts get in the way. As an ER nurse in a tiny town like Willow Brook, I treated many patients who were personal friends and family. It came with the job. I usually didn't think much of it, but dealing with Nate was going to test my limits.

After our last close encounter, well, I'd done my best to avoid anything more than a passing interaction with him. Which was no easy feat, I might add. He was friends with all of my closest friends, my brother's best friend, and his sister-in-law happened to be *my* best friend.

I paused in front of the door of an empty exam room, gesturing him in. "Come on in. I'll take a look and see if we need to order an x-ray."

He slipped into a chair by the counter running along the wall. When I sat down in a wheeled chair and spun to face him, he held his hand up. Reaching out, I carefully cradled it in mine. It was warm to the touch and swollen around his knuckles. "What happened?"

I glanced up into his eyes, and a *zing* of electricity zapped through me. Sweet hell. Those eyes—dark and dangerous and always with a teasing glint.

He lifted his shoulder in a shrug. "I was doing some work on my plane and accidentally knocked loose the blocks around a tire, and one of the wheels rolled over my hand. Hurt like hell. I ignored it at first and just kept working. Now it's pretty swollen, in case you didn't notice," he said with a low chuckle.

"Oh, I noticed. On a scale of one to ten—I'm serious now—where would you rate your pain?" I asked as I gently probed, trying to feel if anything was broken. Unfortunately, the swelling was bad enough, it was hard to tell.

I set his hand down gently on the armrest of his chair, turning away to spin the laptop on its wheeled stand closer to me.

"Maybe a five," he offered.

"Just a five?"

"I'm taking that scale seriously," he said, his laugh belying his comment. "I figure a ten would be like I've been shot, or severely burned, or something like that. Don't get me wrong, it fucking hurts. It's throbbing, and I sure as hell hope you're going to send me home with something for the pain, so I can at least sleep tonight. I'll survive though, so I'm sticking with a five."

I couldn't help but smile in return. "Fair enough, sounds like a five. Hang on." I clicked into the right screen on the computer, tapping on the microphone to call down to radiology. "Hey Tad," I said as soon as he picked up. "I've got Nate Fox up here, and we need to do an x-ray on his hand. Based on the swelling, I can't tell if he broke it or just severely bruised it. I don't want to mess with it too much because it's pretty swollen."

Tad's laugh came through the line. "Let me guess, Nate decided to wait before he came in?"

Tad went to high school with Nate and me, so we all knew each other.

Nate called over. "Hell yeah, I waited. Now I feel like an idiot though, so feel free to give me some shit."

"I'm finishing up with someone else, so give me about ten minutes," Tad replied.

"Got it." I tapped the speaker button to end the call. "So, we wait a few minutes, and then I'll send you downstairs to radiology."

Nate's gaze slid sideways, catching mine. For a flash, heat spun through me. Then he winked, promptly sending my belly into a spinning flip. I turned away quickly, standing and sliding my laptop on the counter. Anything to give me a little space from him. I forced my attention to the electronic chart and made a few entries, speaking as I typed. "Dr. Lane will probably send you home with something for the pain, but you'll need to wait until you get home to take it."

When I glanced over, Nate narrowed his eyes. "If you think I should take my pain medicine now and you'll offer me a ride home, I'll do whatever you say," he said, his voice low and weighted with meaning.

"No thanks," I said quickly, pointedly ignoring the little thrill that raced through me at the heated look in his eyes.

Nate stood from his chair. In one stride, he was right in front of me. I was trapped between him and the counter, with nowhere to go. He set both hands on either side of me, resting his bruised hand on the top of the counter and effectively caging me in his arms.

My pulse went wild and my breath hitched, heat spinning through my veins.

"We have unfinished business," he said flatly.

Scrambling for purchase in my mind and body—my traitorous body, with my nipples perking up and all but begging for Nate's attention—I tried to take a breath and barely managed to get any oxygen. His eyes flicked down to my coffee-stained scrubs then back up, the knowing glint in them only serving to notch up the heat inside.

"I don't know what you're talking about," I finally managed to say, lying through my teeth.

Nate smirked and pissed me right off.

"We kissed. That was it," I muttered.

"Oh Holly," he said, *tsking*. "That wasn't just a kiss. You want me, and I want you. Let's just face up to it and do something about it."

Gah!

See, the problem was I didn't just want Nate. I had a crazy, mad crush on him, but I sure as hell didn't want to admit it. He was more than just sexy to me. He made me want things I knew would be a colossal mess. We had too many shared friends in common. Willow Brook was too small for us to navigate those tricky waters and try something stupid like "friends with benefits."

I had already survived the tragic death of my high school

boyfriend years back and managed to get through it. It's hard to do that in a small town because you can never escape that everybody knows what's going on. I sure as hell didn't think I could escape letting myself fall into the madness between Nate and me when I knew all he wanted was a quick fling.

Nate Fox was practically a professional at quickies. He wasn't an asshole, but he certainly didn't do serious.

I was starting to feel like I was staring down being single for the rest of my life. With one friend after another falling like dominoes—falling in love, getting married, and having babies—I was feeling a little out of the loop these days.

As I stood there with Nate, his hard, muscled body an unholy temptation, I absorbed him for a moment—his rich brown hair and espresso eyes. Nature had been too generous with Nate. He had a square jaw with a dimple in the center of his chin. For God's sake, he even had a dimple in one cheek when he grinned. His nose was slightly crooked from being broken once when he fell off his bike when he was a kid.

See, when you grew up with somebody, you knew all the little details. I'd actually had a little crush on him back in high school. He never even looked twice at me then. We were friends and nothing more. His older brother, Caleb, had been dating my best friend, Ella. Caleb's best friend, Jake, and I ended up getting thrown together all the time as a result, and we eventually started dating. I liked Jake, and we had fun together, but there had never been any thought that he was the love of my life. Then, Jake died in a fiery car crash, and I wasn't sure how to come back from that.

I was saved by the sound of my name being called over the speakers. I swallowed, relieved when Nate stepped back. "Radiology is downstairs. Just take the elevator and follow the signs. Tad will tell you where to go after that," I said quickly.

After I sent Nate off to radiology, I figured I was done

with him for the evening. Tad would send Nate on to the doctor next. I threw myself into dealing with the next patient. This guy had apparently decided to work alone in his garage with a skill-saw and almost cut his finger off. Because, you know, it's smart to take the safety guard off.

Chapter Four

HOLLY

It was a good hour later when I walked down the hallway at the end of my shift. Willow Brook Hospital was a whopping three stories tall. The ER was actually on the second floor because of the way the hospital was built into a hillside, with the parking for the emergency level on the second floor. The lower floor was partially underground, although staff parking was on the lowest floor at the far end of the hospital.

Stepping into the elevator, I was startled to see Nate. I assumed he was long gone by this point. My heart started pounding wildly the moment my eyes landed on him. It was late now, a solid hour past midnight. No one else was in the elevator.

His mouth kicked up at the corner in a sly grin. "Well, hello again. I'm all done for the night. Nothing broken, just badly bruised," he said, holding up his hand, which was in a brace. "They want me to wear this so I don't aggravate it more with too much motion."

I tried to order my heart to slow down, but it willfully ignored me, banging against my ribs while heat spun through my veins. I thought I was in bad shape after Nate and I had our moment in the closet well over a year ago now. But I'd gotten things under control, and then that stupid fundraiser happened.

That was last October on Halloween. We were in the middle of January now. I hadn't forgotten what he said when he walked away that night. The ball was in my court. Nate paid five thousand dollars for a date with me. It shouldn't have been a big deal, but I hadn't been able to scramble up the nerve to approach him about it since then. I'd worked it up into a giant *thing* in my brain.

And now, here we were, trapped in an elevator. Alone.

Coward that I was, I asked, "Were you getting off at this floor?"

Nate's dark eyes narrowed. I felt as if he could see straight through me, into all of my muddled insecurities. He shook his head. "No."

Reaching past me with his good hand, he jabbed the button to close the doors and then promptly hit the button to pause the elevator. In a flash, he was beside me. I curled my hands around the narrow bar encircling the walls inside the elevator, hanging on as if it would save me.

I could feel the heat and strength of him. If I thought my heart was beating fast before, it took off at a full-on gallop now. My breath came in shallow pants and my belly spun, heat blooming through me from head to toe. I knew my cheeks were bright pink because my face was hot. My lower belly clenched, and I tried to catch my breath.

Nate moved with purpose and deliberation, placing one hand and then the other on either side of me. His braced hand rested lightly against the metal bar, while the other curled around it. I looked up and his eyes met mine, his rich brown gaze coasting over my face. He was close enough that when I tried to take a deep breath, my breasts pressed against his chest.

"So..." he drawled. "It looks to me like you're chickening out."

I wanted to protest, to argue the point that I didn't know what he was talking about. But I knew perfectly well what he meant. I practically got skid marks on my tongue to keep from arguing. After a moment, I managed to gather my wits.

"No, I'm not. I'm just waiting for the right time," I muttered with a lift of my chin.

Liar, liar, pants on fire.

"Oh really? And just when do you think will be the right time?"

"Look, if you want a refund, I'll call the fundraiser and explain that I totally screwed up. Or better yet, I'll just reimburse you myself."

"That's insane. You don't have five grand lying around."

He was quite right. My offer was nothing more than a sign of my desperation. I didn't think I could do this. I might've had the hots for Nate for years now, but I couldn't take the way it would go.

Nate was a player. Plain and simple. I'd known him forever. Seeing as he was my twin brother's best friend, I was quite aware of his dating habits, or lack thereof. I wasn't looking for casual. I also wasn't looking to get my heart broken. I liked Nate *way* too much to think we could do some kind of ridiculous "friends with benefits" arrangement. It simply would *not* work.

"It's not about the money, Holly," Nate added, his tone low and sending a hot shiver through me.

I swallowed, trying to get a decent amount of air in my lungs. I only succeeded in having my breasts brush against his chest again, well aware he could likely feel the tight points of my nipples. They were practically waving, standing up and saying hello, entirely without my permission.

I meant to argue the point, to insist he let me reimburse him with money I didn't even have. I opened my mouth to speak and nothing came out. Although, to be fair, it wasn't as if I was all that capable of speech at the moment. Rather, my body was spinning wildly, hot all over, with my panties drenched. This was so embarrassing. Much to my chagrin, I knew Nate had a reputation for being quite skilled in bed. Willow Brook wasn't that big, and he cut a wide swath through the single women in town, along with the tourists who flocked here in the summers.

As I struggled to formulate some sort of sense, he uncurled his good hand from the bar, lifting it and sifting his fingers through my hair. He brushed a few loose tendrils away from my forehead and down behind my ear, goose bumps chasing in the wake of his touch when his fingers brushed against my skin.

"You're afraid," he murmured.

I shook my head wildly, angry and more turned on than I'd ever been in my life.

"Okay, then prove you're not."

"Fine," I finally said, my anger driving me. It lashed at me like a whip, mingling with my inconvenient desire and making me simply wild inside, so hot and bothered I could barely think. "You'll get your date. Dinner at Susitna Burgers & Brew in Anchorage. Valentine's Day."

Nate's eyes widened slightly before darkening. "Okay, maybe you're not a chicken after all," he murmured, right before he leaned forward and brushed his lips across mine.

That subtle touch was a hot sizzle, my lips tingling as he drew back slightly, no more than an inch. On the heels of a muttered imprecation, he fit his mouth over mine again.

Oh. My. God.

There was kissing, and then there was this. The moment Nate angled his head and swept his tongue in my mouth, I was lost. His tongue slid against mine, every stroke sending me spiraling tighter and tighter inside. His hand slid through the ends of my hair, down my shoulder, lightly teasing over my breasts and cupping one through the thin fabric of my scrubs.

When his thumb brushed across the aching peak of a nipple, I moaned into his mouth, gasping when he stepped closer and I could feel the heat of his arousal pressing against my lower belly. Our kiss went wild. With a low growl, he tore his lips free of mine, dusting kisses along my jawline, nipping my earlobe and sending a shudder through me. I couldn't get enough. It wasn't as if I didn't know Nate was all muscle, all man, but to have his body against mine, his hard, muscled chest, the feel of his back flexing as he shifted against me—sweet hell, I was done for.

He made me crazy. I was panting and gasping, my hips rocking into him as his knee slipped between my thighs.

"Fuck, Holly," he muttered, the motion of his lips a tease against the sensitive skin along my neck as he kissed his way down into the valley between my breasts.

I lost sight of everything, awash in sensation as he slid a hand up under my shirt. Somewhere along the way, he shoved my shirt up, bending low to swirl his tongue around one nipple and then the other, right through the silk of my bra. Slick moisture built at my core, a sweet ache growing.

I distantly heard my voice gasping his name, pleading for more.

"I need to touch you," he growled with a nip of his teeth over a nipple.

His hand coasted over the curve of my belly. While I'd never argue that scrubs were sexy, they sure made access easy. With a tug on the messy tie at my waist, he slipped his hand down between my thighs. I didn't even hesitate, my legs parting wider when he nudged a knee out to the side. He trailed his fingers over the wet silk there, and I bit back a moan.

I wasn't thinking. *At all*. All I knew was I needed this not to stop. Blessedly, Nate appeared to be on the same page. Another tease over the silk and then he pushed it aside, sinking one and then two fingers in my drenched channel. I was dripping wet—for him. I felt him lift his head where he'd been teasing his lips along my collarbone.

"Holly," he murmured, his voice alone throwing another hot spark into the fire raging inside of me.

Dragging my eyes open, I found his dark gaze waiting. He proceeded to drive me straight to the edge with his fingers. I forgot everything—where we were, all the rational reasons why I shouldn't let this happen, how I hated feeling this vulnerable with anyone, much less with him. I chased after that sweet release, crying out when he swirled his thumb over my swollen clit as he drove his fingers deep inside me.

If it was actually possible for someone to fuck you with a look, somehow Nate had pulled that off. The searing heat of his gaze fed right into my climax as it rippled through me, pleasure scattering in scorching sparks. My head fell against the wall of the elevator as I struggled to catch my breath.

Nate slowly withdrew his hand, his eyes on me the entire time. I was fairly certain I'd have melted to the floor if he hadn't been holding me up. He even tied the waistband of my not-so-sexy scrub pants and straightened my shirt. Just as my brain was flickering back to sanity, there was a loud crackle, and then a voice came over the speaker in the elevator. "Testing, testing. Is everything okay, or is the elevator stuck?" a male voice asked.

"Oh my God," I muttered.

Nate found it funny, his gaze catching mine as his lips curled in a grin that only sent another hot jolt of need through me, making me acutely aware of what had just happened.

I pushed at his chest. A lost cause because he didn't move.

Lifting his head, he replied to whoever was on the other end of the speaker. "Everything's fine." He reached over to tap the button for the elevator to move, finally stepping away from me.

The reality of what had just transpired slammed into me.

Thank God there were no cameras in this elevator. Not that
I knew of.

Oh great, something else you can obsess about.

The ride to the ground floor was silent. When we
stepped out, Nate's hand rested at the base of my spine. I
couldn't bring myself to speak, much less swat his hand away.
That was the problem with me when it came to him. Every
time we touched, all I wanted was *more*.

My jacket was looped over my arm, and I gripped it
tightly. I paused by the doors, finally stepping away from
him and shrugging into it, zipping it up quickly. My nipples
were still tight, so tight they ached.

With my cheeks still flaming hot, I met his gaze. "Well,
I'm sure I'll see you around," I finally said.

"Of course. I'll call you the day before Valentine's Day."

Four long weeks stretched before me.

Chapter Five

NATE

I angled the plane slightly as I flew through the air, aiming in the direction of Denali, far ahead in the distance. I had the best damn job in the world. I flew planes and helicopters all over Alaska, sometimes for tourists, sometimes for transport, and sometimes just for fun.

Statistically speaking, my job was risky. Aviation accidents in Alaska bounced around from year to year, but had hovered at about twice the national average for years. I loved it, though, and the risk was worth it to me. Any day I was up in the air, the wilderness was splashed in front of me. The natural cathedral of Alaska was breathtaking. Mountains, the sun breaking through the clouds, glaciers, miles and miles of uninterrupted forest, rivers sparkling under the sun, and the ocean, all serving to remind you of just how small you were in the universe.

Despite the risks, I didn't love flying for the rush. I loved it for the sense of freedom it gave me. Another thing was the pay was damn good, and I was largely my own boss. I ran a small aviation company based out of Willow Brook and partnered with a few of the bigger companies in Anchorage.

During the summer, every single day was different. There was nothing monotonous about my work. Sometimes, I ran flights to pick up firefighter crews, or dropped fire retardant over fires. Other days, I ferried tourists to and from fishing and hunting locations. Yet other days, I simply took people out flightseeing.

I angled the plane slowly as I saw the remote lodge coming into view ahead, situated on the edge of a picturesque lake in the middle of freaking nowhere Alaska. As the crow flew, it was only about two hours north and west of Willow Brook. Any other way here was a grueling trip over rugged terrain in complete wilderness.

The concept of a runway in Alaska was quite different than in most areas. In remote areas, it could be a gravel strip of land, or a grassy field, or a lake. This place actually had a gravel strip about a half a mile long, just enough for me to land. In the winter, it could be dicey, but the weather had been on our side and the lodge owners maintained this airstrip pretty well.

When I flew helicopters out in the backcountry for fire-fighters, I'd had to learn to land on a dime in all kinds of conditions to get people in and out safely. I loved the precision of it. Setting my plane down with a light touch, I slowed and came to a stop at the edge of the runway. The wind was down today, which was always good. Some days, I felt like I was flying in a clothes dryer with the small plane easily buffeted by the wind.

Once I was on the ground, it didn't take too long for me to load everybody up in the plane. This lodge served those hardcore outdoor types. In the winter, that usually meant backcountry skiers. This group was a friendly crew, helping me get everything loaded up before we took off.

A few hours later, I was back in Willow Brook, locking up the plane hangar and walking outside to my truck. I owned the land and several hangars on the outskirts of Willow Brook. I'd saved up the money during my first few years of flying, and now rented out hangar space to other pilots in the area.

As I stepped into the chilly evening air, the sun was setting, staining the sky pink and lavender. I was meeting my brother and some friends at Wildlands, a popular local hangout and a busy tourist attraction during the summer.

The lights were on at a few shops as I drove through downtown Willow Brook and turned onto the side road that ran parallel to Main Street, Swan Lake Road. Swan Lake, the centerpiece of Willow Brook, glimmered under the setting sun. It was a sprawling lake, host to all kinds of wildlife, most specifically a breeding ground for Trumpeter swans, the lake's namesake. The lake was surrounded with hunting lodges and a few smaller homes, most of them closed up during the winter. Wildlands, on the other hand, was open year-round.

The parking lot behind the massive timber frame style lodge was almost at capacity. Squeezing my truck in a corner space, I pocketed my keys as I walked in through the back entrance. Warmth and the low hum of voices surrounded me as I strode down the hallway into the bar and restaurant area.

Well-worn hardwood floors and exposed beams show-cased the practical, inviting space. The owners kept it simple with wooden tables and booths, pool tables over to one side, and a small stage on the opposite end for the music acts that passed through town during the summer.

The bar area was always more crowded, but even the restaurant was full tonight. Scanning the crowd, my eyes landed on Holly's bright blonde hair. Of course she would be here. We ran in the same circles, which only made my attraction to her that much more inconvenient. Anticipation thrummed in my body, like that of an engine revving. It had been a mere three days since our interlude at the hospital, when it had taken all of my discipline not to fuck her against the wall of the elevator.

Threading my way through the crowd, I aimed straight for Holly because I knew that was where my brother would be, and most likely Holly's twin brother, Alex. This thing I had for Holly stretched back much further than she knew. We'd grown up together, our small worlds overlapping in Willow Brook. It wasn't until high school that I first noticed she wasn't just my best buddy's annoying sister. Alex predictably teased her, and I went along with it. When we were kids, I didn't think about it much, not back then. Growing up, Holly had been willful, opinionated, and tomboy as all hell.

In high school, like a bolt of lightning one day, I looked at her and wanted her. Fiercely. She'd always been a bit ahead of the curve as far as development, but all of a sudden, one day, I noticed she had quite generous breasts and a lush ass. With her twin brother and me practically inseparable, I was often at their house. She pranced around in tank tops and cut-off sweatpants, not realizing they showed off her assets far too well.

Years later now, I couldn't say it was much more than lust. Hell, teenage boys were practically led around by their cocks. I never acted on it. For starters, there was a complication of her brother being my best friend, and then she started dating Jake Green. I never knew just how much he meant to her, but I sure liked teasing her about him. And then everything blew up.

An icy highway in Alaska, a drunk driver coming the opposite direction, and four kids in a fiery car accident—my older brother, Caleb, his girlfriend and Holly's best friend, Ella, Holly, and Jake.

Jake died when he was thrown from the vehicle. Everyone else survived, although Ella came damn close to not pulling through and likely would have died if Caleb hadn't pulled her out of the wreckage.

The accident sent painful reverberations through the small world of Willow Brook. It had been shocking. One day,

Jake was alive, and the next morning, we all learned he was dead. Meanwhile, Ella clung to life in the burn unit in Anchorage for weeks.

Holly had sustained a few bumps and bruises. Caleb came out with nothing more than a few scrapes, while he spiraled emotionally when Ella broke up with him. They were back together now, but it had taken years for them to cross that bridge.

All the fun stuff about being a teenager was put on hold for any of us close to the emotional blast radius of that accident. Holly and I kept a polite distance. To say I hadn't known how to comfort anyone in that situation was a massive understatement. I just tried not to upset anyone— not Caleb, not Ella, and certainly not Holly. Teasing, my go-to response for everything back then and now, had felt completely wrong.

Holly had stayed in Willow Brook, only leaving temporarily while she went to nursing school in Anchorage. I went to flight school, focusing on getting my pilot's license to fly small planes and helicopters. Things shifted between us, and I had ordered my body to stop lusting after her.

That had been years ago. All bets were off now. When I approached the large round table, I noticed the only empty chair happened to be beside Holly. Score. Slipping into it, I scanned the table. Caleb was here with his arm draped around Ella's shoulders. Caleb and I shared the same brown hair and eyes, while Ella had dark brown hair and green eyes. For the first time in years, Caleb seemed back to himself.

That accident had nearly torn him apart. His best friend had died and his girlfriend had come too damn close. Ella and Caleb were those rare people who met young, and you just knew they were meant to be together, even then. I'd been so damn relieved when they finally got back together. Now I could tease him again.

Cade Masters, Ella's older brother, was there, along with his wife, Amelia. A few hotshot firefighters were there, as well as one of Holly's friends, Rachel Garrett, a medical assistant.

I grinned when Caleb called over, "Hey, how was the flight?"

"Uneventful, exactly how I like them. The wind was down, which isn't always the case when it's sunny, so that was a win."

A waiter stopped by the table, and I ordered a beer and a burger, glancing down at Holly's almost empty wine glass. "Need a refill?" I asked.

Her wide brown eyes swung up to mine. My body tensed instantly, that low hum of anticipation rising a notch.

"Sure," she replied, glancing up to the waiter and lifting her glass.

"Be right back with that," he said as he turned away.

"How's it going?" I asked.

Holly's cheeks pinkened as she looked up at me. It did *not* help matters, not one bit, that I knew what her lips felt like under mine. The memory of it was quite fresh. She had plump, full lips, and a teasing tongue I just knew would drive me wild swirling around my cock.

The things I wanted to do to Holly Blake weren't appropriate thoughts for the moment.

"Fine," she said, her voice coming out husky. She quickly gulped down the last bit of her wine.

"How about you?"

"Same. Less than a month until Valentine's Day," I replied with a grin.

Her cheeks flushed even pinker. Hot damn, I wanted to kiss her.

"What are you doing?" she hissed.

I couldn't help but grin. I suspected Holly wanted to keep our upcoming date a secret, a very well-kept secret. Although I wasn't up for our tight knit circle of friends knowing all about it, I sure as hell didn't mind teasing her about it.

Leaning an elbow on the table, I curled my other hand over her thigh, feeling the heat of her skin through the denim. "What?" I asked innocently.

"What are you doing?" she repeated, her tone low and fierce.

"What do you think?" I murmured as I slid my hand up her thigh. She shifted her legs and cast a glare in my direction. Although I was getting a kick out of teasing her, I underestimated my body's own reaction to being close to her. My cock swelled, pressing against the buttons of my fly.

Because it was Holly, and because somehow we'd tumbled back to a place where I couldn't help but challenge her, I stubbornly left my hand on her thigh, my thumb brushing back and forth. The temptation to slide further up and feel the sweet heat of her core was strong.

That was the thing that was making me so damn crazy about Holly. I didn't do things like this. I had flings—brief, casual, and *always* under control. Holly snatched my control.

Cade said something, dragging my attention away from Holly. Conversation carried around us while I was only half-focused. My beer arrived, followed by my burger, and only then did I actually remove my hand from her. For God's sake, the fact that simply touching her thigh had made me this turned on was saying something.

Holly was busy talking to Amelia when Ella made a comment directed at me.

"Oh, well that's Nate's job," she said, tossing a teasing grin my way.

"Nate's job?" Caleb's question came next.

"The local player," Ella said with a little laugh. "Come to think of it though, you've been falling down on the job."

I felt Holly's gaze swing to me. Normally, I would take this in stride, but I was caught just now. I wanted to play it cool and pass this off with a laugh. Yet, the last thing I wanted was for Holly to think that was still my thing. Even

more, I didn't want her to read too much into us. I figured
that would send her running.

With a few too many eyes at the table on me, I simply
shrugged and laughed. "I'm not that much of a player."

I felt my brother's gaze on me, his eyes narrowing. Caleb
had actually commented on this very thing the other day.
He'd never hesitated to give me shit. He had maintained the
role of the responsible older brother quite well. In some
ways, the tragedy of his best friend from high school dying
and Ella almost dying had kicked the laugh right out of
Caleb for a few years. He was getting it back, but he'd never
been one to play the joker.

Whether it was in reaction to events or not, I'd assumed
that role in our family, in more ways than one.

"Well, you settle down and then maybe I'll believe it,"
Ella said with another laugh. Lately, she'd been on my case as
well, telling me I was going to miss out on the right person if
I refused to consider anything serious. Seeing as Holly was
her best friend, I wasn't about to tell Ella that I was
distracted and restless and not able to even notice another
woman entirely because of Holly.

In fact, I hadn't had sex since before last Halloween.
Unlike last year after our unexpected make out session in the
closet when we were both a little too drunk, I hadn't been
able to shake the effect of Holly on me this time.

"All right, well, then maybe you'll believe it sometime," I
replied easily.

Caleb simply rolled his eyes and shook his head while
Ella patted my shoulder. I loved my friends and loved my
family, but I didn't love how damn nosy they could be. Blessedly, conversation moved on when the waiter stopped by to
gather empty plates and see if anybody needed anything else.

Chapter Six

HOLLY

My cheeks were hot, my panties were wet, and my pulse just wouldn't quit. Not that I wanted it to quit, mind you. That would've meant I was having a heart attack. Although, I suppose Nate was the most likely person to cause me to have a heart attack.

I needed to escape. With him here beside me, his heat and strength emanating, and the woodsy scent he carried drifting to me, I was all kinds of hot and bothered. I took a shaky breath, letting it out slowly. When Charlie stood to go, I snagged my jacket off the back of my chair.

"I need to get going too," I said brightly.

Not bothering to wait for a round of goodbyes, I blew a kiss at the table in general and spun away, hurrying to catch up with Charlie. She glanced over her shoulder, her gray eyes meeting mine. "You okay?" she asked.

I wanted to say, *"No, not at all. I want to fuck one of my best friends, or someone who used to be one of my best friends, but we grew apart because life does that when things get weird. But I can't. It doesn't make any sense because he's a player, and I can't just be another in his long list of women. He'll break my heart, and I already know it."*

Those words stayed locked in my mind with my biggest secret nagging at me. I was a virgin. It was a heavy weight to carry. No one knew, and probably everybody would be shocked.

All of these thoughts stumbled through my mind as I looked at Charlie. We had come to a stop near the bar where a narrow hallway led to the back parking lot.

"Are you okay, Holly?" she repeated. This time, her voice held more than passing concern. I didn't know what she saw in my expression, but she looked downright worried.

I nodded quickly. "Oh yeah, I'm fine, just a little tired."

Charlie regarded me for another moment, the hum of voices around us carrying on. After a beat, she gave my shoulder a squeeze and resumed walking, her dark hair swinging between her shoulders as she walked ahead of me down the hallway. I wondered what Charlie would think if she knew about my unintended virginal state. I doubted she would laugh because she was too kind for that, but I was pretty sure she'd be damn surprised. I was myself.

Charlie was a doctor, and I worked with her occasionally at the hospital. We'd become friends through work and our social circles bumping into each other once she got serious with Jesse Franklin, a hotshot firefighter who happened to be friends with many of my friends. I loved how down to earth Charlie was. She'd been through her own series of challenges—taking care of her mother with dementia and adopting her niece after her sister died from cancer. She certainly understood that life was complicated, but she took it in stride.

Somehow, I always found it easier to be there for my friends—to be the strong one, the funny one—than to let them know just how out of whack I felt inside sometimes. With a mental shake, I paused beside the bathroom in the hall, calling out to Charlie who was a few strides ahead of me. "Bathroom break before I drive home. I'll probably see you at the hospital in the next few days, okay?"

Charlie glanced back, flashing a smile. "Of course. I'm on call Friday."

Stepping into the bathroom, I closed the door and leaned against it, taking a few deep breaths. I went to the bathroom quickly. After washing my hands in the sink, I splashed some water on my face. My cheeks were hot, and I needed to cool down. Hell, I was hot all over, but then, that was the effect Nate had on me.

I was seriously considering how to get out of the stupid date with him. It was bad enough I couldn't seem to kick him out of my mind. Ever since that stupid kiss at that party —all because I'd had a little too much champagne—I hadn't been able to stop thinking about it. Then, that fundraiser happened, and he kissed me. Again.

And then *again* in the elevator. Oh God. I splashed more water on my face. Just thinking about what happened in the elevator pretty much set me on fire. Kisses with Nate were a terrible idea for me. He was too damn good at it. He was in his own category when it came to driving me absolutely wild. Even though I was a virgin, I had no shortage of experience with everything that led up to the main act, so to speak.

After the accident in high school, all the guys in town kept about a mile away from me. Everyone assumed I was heartbroken and devastated. And I was, but not in the way everybody thought. Jake and I had sort of fallen into dating. With Jake being Caleb's best friend and Ella mine, we were thrown together all the time. It was high school, and we were young. We'd been friends for years as it was. Like I had told Ella many times after she and Caleb broke up and before they found their way back to each other, not everyone found the kind of love they had when they were young.

Especially not in high school. Most of us were just stumbling along, with our hormones sending confusing signals. By virtue of our two best friends falling madly in love and spending every minute together, Jake and I were together a lot. So, we started dating. He was my friend, and I cared about him. I was devastated when he died, but not because he'd been the love of my life. What a confusing heartbreak it was.

The whole town, or that was how it felt, assumed our love had been devastatingly cut short. When it really was more a *friendship* that had been brutally cut short. Because of the genuine tragedy of Jake's death, everyone made all kinds of assumptions. Meanwhile, I was grief-stricken and my best friend almost died on top of it. All three of us had survivor's guilt. While Ella had fled from it, I faced it head-on and got through to the other side. I was truly okay, yet I never got around to correcting the assumption everyone made about Jake and me. It was what it was, and it felt weird to go out of my way to say we'd mostly been friends after it all.

By the time I was in the mood to have fun and date again, I somehow missed out on ditching my virginity. I was a freaking virgin at the age of twenty-eight. It was a bit of a burden and more annoying than anything. At this stage in my life, I was well aware most men would be surprised to learn I was still one.

Either I lied by omission and didn't tell anyone I was a virgin, and it was maybe a little awkward if things got that far, or I told them the truth, and they ran screaming the other way. Because who wanted to deal with a twenty-eight-year-old virgin? Certainly not me. I didn't even want to deal with myself about it.

After another splash of cold water on my face, I dabbed my face with a towel, dried my hands, and stepped out of the bathroom. Only to run smack into Nate walking down the hallway.

Fuck, fuck, fuck.

He glanced down, his eyes darkening the moment they met mine. "I thought you left," he said.

I reached down and zipped up my jacket as I stepped back, heat flooding through me all over again. "I'm leaving right now," I said quickly. I strolled past him, tucking my hands into my jacket sleeves and gripping the cuffs, as if that would somehow keep me from latching onto him.

Nate caught up to me quickly. I could feel his presence behind me as his hand reached out, curling around the handle of the door and pulling it open for me. My eyes flicked down, watching his strong fingers, coasting over a few scars on his knuckles. He had good hands—strong and rugged. A shiver ran through me as I recalled the feel of his fingers inside me.

It suddenly occurred to me he wasn't wearing the brace on his hand anymore. "Where's your brace?" I asked, almost relieved for something to say that had nothing to do with the mad desire spinning inside me.

"Hand feels fine. Charlie only told me to wear it until it felt better, so that's what I did," he replied with a quick shrug.

"Oh."

"You sure you don't want to lecture me on it?" he asked, his lips curling into a sly grin.

Rolling my eyes, I shook my head and hurried past him, the cold winter air a welcome relief as it hit my skin. "Good night," I called over my shoulder. I could practically feel his gaze boring into my back as I hurried across the parking lot and jumped in my car.

On the drive home, through the winter night with the silver light of the moon cast over the snowy landscape, I resolved to myself that I would call Nate tomorrow and tell him we just couldn't do this. I wanted him too much, and I wanted more than I knew he was willing to offer.

Chapter Seven

HOLLY

Staring into the kitchen pantry the next morning, I stared up at the empty spot on the shelf where I should've had a bag of coffee beans. Shit. I looked hopefully toward the coffee grinder sitting innocently beside the espresso maker on my kitchen counter. I strode to it, pulling out the bin to see if maybe there was enough coffee for a cup in there. No such luck. There was maybe enough for a thimbleful of coffee. Most definitely not enough to start my day.

I sighed. So much for a leisurely morning before I went into work. I needed coffee, and I needed it now. I had a shitty night's sleep. I'd arrived home hot and bothered after spending too much time in Nate's proximity. I tried to talk my body down, but I finally gave in and used my trusty vibrator to take care of matters. Unfortunately, the only man who passed through my thoughts when my climax crashed over me was Nate.

My kitchen was a bit of a mess too. I had hoped for enough time to clean up this morning. There were a few too many dishes piled in my sink, and I needed to start a load of laundry. I lived alone in a small apartment above an office supply business, and the windows looked out over Main Street in downtown Willow Brook. My kitchen was cute, with a small island with stools for seating, and pretty slate blue tile on the counters and the floor, the white birch cabinets brightening the space.

The kitchen faced the living room, which had a small sectional with plenty of cushions, a television mounted on the side wall, and a view of Swan Lake in the distance. I had enough money to buy my own place and some property, but it didn't feel right. I wanted to settle down and have a family, and had been resisting actually buying my own home. Somehow, it represented to me the capitulation into permanent single status. I knew it wasn't logical, but it was what it was. I respected the hell out of women who chose to live independently and on their own terms, but I wanted a shot at a relationship.

With a sigh, I padded across the hardwood floor in the living room, running a hand through my messy hair, and stepped into the small bedroom. This was definitely a one-person apartment with the kitchen and living room together, and one giant bedroom with a single bathroom.

I needed coffee more than I needed a morning to myself. After rushing through a shower, I tossed all the dishes in the dishwasher, then threw the laundry in the washer and put it on a delayed start before I left to walk down to Firehouse Café.

The café was conveniently right down the street. I bundled up so the icy winter morning didn't bother me too much. The air wasn't quite as good as coffee, but it certainly woke me up.

Willow Brook was a pretty little town in the winter with Swan Lake iced over, and the marks of skis and ice skates crisscrossing its surface. The mountains stood sentry in the distance, their tall, snowcapped peaks shimmering against the horizon. In some elevated parts of town, the ocean was visible. It was about a half an hour drive south. With

Anchorage roughly an hour east and the wilderness stretching out beyond Willow Brook, it felt as if the little town was a world unto itself in the winter. I suppose it was.

Come summer, the world came to Willow Brook in the form of hikers, bikers, hunters, and more, all vying for a slice of Alaska's beauty. The storefronts along Willow Brook's Main Street were a mix of small restaurants and shopping, mostly outdoor gear and arts, and a few choice coffee shops. Firehouse Café loomed ahead on the corner of Main Street and another cross street. It was aptly named as it was housed in the town's original fire station. Years back, the small town had built an improved fire station to serve as a hub for the region. The old fire station was in a square, two-story brick building.

The outside of the café had been spruced up with a mural painted along one corner of the brick and brightly-colored accents of pink and purple on the window frames. Entering through the bright purple door, the old garage space had been transformed into a seating area with the open kitchen and deli to the side, and a bakery area through a swinging door in the back.

Janet James' family had moved here back in the days of homesteading. She and her husband had established Firehouse Café and a few other businesses years back. Her husband had since died in a car accident on an icy highway up north. Janet had stayed strong and still ran Firehouse Café. She was a mainstay in Willow Brook, and I couldn't imagine her not being here.

Warmth enveloped me when I stepped through the door, along with the hum of voices and the scent of fresh coffee and baked goods. The space was open and airy with a pressed tin ceiling and the old fire pole still in the center of the room. The concrete floor had been stained a soft blue. The café was cheerful with fireweed flowers, Alaska's spectacularly beautiful weed, decorating the fire pole, and artwork mounted on the walls with brightly painted windowsills and cheerful curtains. Small square tables were scattered about the space.

I aimed straight for the line at the deli counter. A chalkboard with the regular menu and daily specials hung above. As I contemplated whether to get the house coffee or one of Janet's double chocolate coffees, I heard my name. Glancing over my shoulder, I smiled when I saw my twin brother, Alex. We shared the same blond hair and brown eyes, but the resemblance ended there. There was the obvious distinction that Alex was a man, and I wasn't. He stood a good foot taller than me and had a lanky build. Somehow, he had lucked out in the twin lottery and could eat whatever he wanted and stay thin.

Meanwhile, all I had to do was *think* about that double chocolate coffee, and I probably gained a pound in the process. I'd learned to accept my curves and fought to remind myself that women didn't need to meet society standards. But still, when it came to curves, I had more than enough to go around.

"Hey, Holl," Alex said, nudging me with his elbow when he reached my side. As usual, he looked as if he'd rolled right out of bed before he showed up here. His hair was mussed, and he wore an unzipped fleece jacket over a gray jersey shirt. Battered jeans topped off his look, with leather boots competing for the most worn item of the day.

"Hey, what brings you here this morning?"

"The coffee, what else?" he replied with a chuckle. "You already headed into the hospital?"

"In a bit. I meant to have a lazy morning this morning, but I was out of coffee at home."

"I'll get yours this morning," he said as we stepped to the front of the line. "I think I owe you one."

Janet beamed at us. As usual, her dark hair streaked with silver was twisted into a braid, which she flicked off her shoulder, and her brown eyes twinkled with her smile. Janet was the kind of person who made you feel better just for existing. She gave off a warm, motherly air with her round build and wide smile, only reinforcing the impression.

"Good morning, you two. I don't get to see you together enough. I forget how much you look alike."

Alex chuckled. "We *are* twins after all."

Janet rolled her eyes. "As if I needed you to remind me. Anyway, what can I get for you two?"

"I'll take the double chocolate coffee," Alex replied, glancing to me.

"I'll take a straight Americano with just a dash of cream."

"Coming right up," Janet said as she spun away and began prepping our coffees.

Daniel, who worked there, paused beside her, quickly filling her in on an issue with one of the baking ovens in the back. She managed to get our coffees and ring us up while walking him through what to do to fix it.

Alex and I stepped away together. "Wanna sit for a few?" Alex asked.

"Of course. I'm sitting anyway. I've got an hour to kill. Oh crap, I need food."

Alex grinned. "I'll get a table, you get your food."

As I turned back and moved to get to the back of the line, Janet called over, "Bagel?"

"Please. And salmon cream cheese," I added.

My hips could take it, or at least that's what I told myself as I turned away.

"Just pay me later," Janet said. "Daniel will bring it over once it's ready."

"Awesome, thanks!" I returned, blowing her a kiss.

Threading my way through the tables, I slipped into a chair across from Alex at a table by the windows. Just as I was about to say something, I heard Alex's name in a distinct voice that lately, I couldn't get out of my head. Specifically, I couldn't get Nate's gruff whisper in the elevator out of my head. *"I need to touch you."*

Things had gone from bad to worse as far as the state of

my body and Nate. Now, it appeared all he had to do was speak, and my pulse lunged and heat spun in my core, radiating outward.

"Hey, man," Alex called.

I spent an inordinate amount of attention adjusting the lid on my coffee and taking a sip. I even opened it to add a bit more cream. Nate reached our table, hooking his hand over a chair and sitting down on the side between us. His knee bumped mine, sending a little *zing* of electricity through me, my skin tingling at the point of contact.

This was beyond ridiculous. I willed my cheeks not to heat as I looked up and tried to keep my expression bland. "Morning, Nate."

He caught my eyes, a teasing grin kicking up the corners of his mouth. "Morning, Holly."

This was why the thing with Nate was a mess for me. He was such a tease that he could do it right here in front of my brother, and Alex likely wouldn't pick up on anything. Because Nate was a flirt and a tease in general. It wasn't specific to me, something I needed to remember. I hoped like hell Alex couldn't tell how flustered I was.

Daniel appeared with my bagel. "Anything else?" he asked, setting the small plate down in front of me.

Nate glanced up. "Don't suppose I can ask you to get me a coffee?" Nate asked. "I'll pay on my way out."

"Of course. What do you need?"

"I'll take the double chocolate."

With a nod, Daniel turned away, and I promptly took a bite of my bagel. If my mouth was full, then I wouldn't have to talk. Alex and Nate launched into their usual banter. Alex was a specialized mechanic for planes. As such, he and Nate often crossed paths in their work. Not to mention they were best friends and hung out on the regular.

I was pretty much stuffing my face to keep from talking when Alex spoke. "Damn, Holly. You hungry, or what?"

I finished chewing and swallowed, taking a sip of coffee before looking up. "It so happens I am."

Alex grinned. Daniel seemed to be in tune with my need for distraction and arrived with Nate's coffee right then.

After he turned away, Alex stood from the table. "I need to get going, actually. I only had a few minutes. I'll catch you both later, okay?"

I lifted my hand in a wave, purposefully not taking another bite so I didn't actually stuff my face too fast. "See ya. Thanks for the coffee."

Nate took a long swallow of coffee and gave a quick wave in response. He slid into the chair across from me once Alex was out of sight. His dark chocolate gaze meandered over me.

Great, fucking awesome. Just what I need. Nate looking at me like that.

I had to tell him we needed to call this little dance off. There would be no date, and there could be absolutely no more kisses, or anything remotely similar to what happened in the elevator. I figured this location was perfect. We weren't alone, so I could make my escape if needed.

I took a gulp of my coffee and eyed him. On the heels of a deep breath, I said, "Here's the deal, I can't go on that date. I'm not sure why you spent that five grand, but if it's a big deal, I promise I'll reimburse you. I know you think it's funny and for some crazy reason, we keep kissing, but I can't do this with you."

Nate's intent gaze never broke away from mine, his eyes narrowing as I spoke. My heart was pounding wildly, and my nerves were on high alert.

"Why?"

Of course. He just *had* to demand to know why. I hadn't thought this far.

I forged ahead. "Look, we've been friends forever. You're Alex's best friend. No matter what, it's going to be awkward.

You're not looking for anything serious, and you never have been. I can't just be..."

I paused, unsure how to say what I meant. After a fortifying gulp of coffee, I continued. "One of your flings. It's totally not my style. I don't want to have things get weird with us. I'm too old for that, and I'd like a shot at finding someone I can get serious with."

Nate went still and quiet, pausing to take a slow sip of his coffee before setting it down on the table. He stared at me for a few beats more than was comfortable. I looked away, stuffing in another bite of bagel and chewing my frustration out.

I hated this situation. Why, oh why did I have to have the hots for my brother's best friend? So, so inconvenient.

When I looked back to Nate, he was still quiet, and I didn't know how to read his expression. After another moment, he cleared his throat and took a gulp of his coffee. With his gaze pinned to mine, he lifted his chin slightly. "Why so serious all of a sudden?"

"Oh my God. This is what I don't want to have to explain. You're Mr. Casual. I would just be another in your long list of women. I don't really feel like it. I'm not so stupid as to pretend like there's nothing between us. But you and I don't want the same thing. If it's a big deal, I'll find a way to pay you back."

His eyes narrowed as he leaned across the table. "It's not about the money. I guess I just didn't take you for a coward."

Oh my fucking God, he pissed me off so much. "I'm not a coward! I just don't want to make things any more complicated than they need to be. You avoided me like the fucking plague after that stupid kiss last year. Then, you show up at the fundraiser and buy a date. What the hell? No thanks. I don't need any of this. Plus, the absolute last person I want to lose my virginity with is *you*," I retorted.

Chapter Eight

HOLLY

Oh dear God. I just told Nate I was a virgin.

The moment my last sentence went strolling out of my mouth—entirely without my permission, by the way—I wanted to snatch it back and run.

Nate's mouth actually fell open. With my cheeks flaming hot, I almost burst out laughing. For a split second, I had the upper hand. I'd managed to surprise the hell out of him. Except now, he knew my biggest, most annoying, secret.

After a moment, he shook his head. "What?" He looked genuinely confused.

I was going to have to breeze my way right through this. Whatever. He might annoy the hell out of me sometimes, and I might wish I didn't want him the way I did, but he wouldn't run his mouth. I took a big gulp of my coffee, savoring the bitterness and wishing I had that kick of dark chocolate to give me a little more courage.

I shrugged, striving for nonchalance. "You heard me. It's not a big deal. It's just..." Pausing, I took a deep breath, letting it out with a sigh. "It was kind of an accident."

"An accident?" Nate countered with another shake of his head, his expression almost dazed.

Fuck it. I let that kind of major detail slip, but whatever. I would just tell him the blunt truth, which would most likely put a screeching halt to whatever the hell he was thinking about us.

"Pretty much. I mean, it's not like I've been saving myself. Anyway, I'd appreciate it if you didn't mention that to anyone."

Nate was still staring at me, his eyes wide. After another beat, he took a giant gulp of coffee, draining what was left in his mug before setting it down. I wished I could climb inside of his brain and see what he was thinking. I'd known him forever, so I could tell the wheels were spinning like mad in his mind.

Janet blessedly paused by the table, winking at me and then looking toward Nate. "Coffee's on me today," she said with a grin.

It took a minute for him to kick into gear and focus on her when he finally tore his gaze free from me before he looked up. "You sure?" he asked with a grin.

Janet nodded, opening her mouth as if to say something else right when someone called her name. She patted him on the shoulder and turned away. I took that moment to make my escape. "Well," I began as I stuffed the last of my bagel in the small pastry bag, "I've got to get to work. Bye."

I hurried away, not even bothering to wait for him to reply. That might've been the most mortifying few minutes of my life. I practically ran down the street to my car where it was parked behind my apartment.

Well, that should put a stop to that disaster in the making. I'm pretty sure Nate doesn't want to be responsible for anybody's virginity, much less mine.

Not that I thought men were responsible for taking anyone's virginity. Women were responsible for their own bodies and choices, but that didn't change the perception around virginity. As for Nate, whose middle name should've been Casual, I was pretty damn sure that wasn't something he wanted any part of.

Part of me was let down. I was so annoyed with the circumstances in my life that had led me to this. I remembered talking to Ella when she finally moved back to Willow Brook. There were some things I had faced head-on after the accident, while she had fled. What I hadn't counted on was every guy in town giving me a wide berth because they assumed I was devastated and heartbroken over my lost high school love. I was, but Jake and I had been good friends who tried to date. I mean, I never even got around to having sex with him!

Ugh. That was what it all boiled down to. This whole situation had me annoyed beyond belief. Why, why, *why* did I have to be so attracted to Nate? Of all people.

I wasn't so stupid as to think that just because the chemistry that flashed to life like a freaking bonfire between us meant it would become something serious. I also wasn't about to set myself up for nothing more than a fling when I knew that wasn't what I wanted. It was just all too complicated.

Once I arrived to work, I was relieved for the distraction. The emergency department at Willow Brook Hospital was always quieter in the winter, but it was still busy. As the head nurse for the ED, when it was busy there, I simply spun from one emergency to the next. When it wasn't insane, I did whatever else needed to be done.

Today, that meant a rotation in the morning on the long-term unit. With Willow Brook being a rural hospital, but in proximity to Anchorage, we had a small collection of patients who needed long-term care. It was essentially a hospice unit.

While some people thought it was depressing, and in some ways, it was sad, I actually enjoyed spending a few hours on the unit. For starters, the patients were often funny as hell and far more philosophical than most. They dispensed life advice freely and without a drop of caution.

When I stepped into Joanna's room, she looked up from her bed when the door clicked shut behind me, a wide smile stretching across her face. Joanna was in her nineties and her adult children had moved out of state, but often came back to visit. Joanna had been dealing with rheumatoid arthritis for years and had significant mobility issues.

"Oh goody, I get you this morning," she said. Her thin, reedy voice belied her cheerful spirit. She had been dwindling lately, and we all worried she might be getting close to the end. The hospital social worker had called her children the other day to let them know. I wasn't sure if Joanna knew they were planning to come visit this weekend.

"Hey, Joanna," I said as I approached her bed. "How's it going this morning?"

"As well as can be expected when I'm wearing an adult diaper," she said with a sly smile, which set off a coughing spree.

"Let me get you something to drink."

Spinning to the tray beside her bed, I poured her preferred apple juice and waited a moment until her coughing subsided. She tapped the button on her remote to raise her bed slightly. On the heels of a shallow breath, she took the small paper cup of apple juice from me and took several sips.

"There, that's better. I'm glad I got you this morning. I didn't sleep well. You won't try to sweet talk me into those meds for my cough that just put me to sleep. I hate sleeping all the time. I figure I'm going to die soon enough, I might as well be awake while I'm alive," she said with a wry grin, just as the door opened and Chris Grant stepped into the room.

Chris was another reason I enjoyed my occasional rotations on this wing . He was another nurse at the hospital, a good friend and funny as hell.

"Well, hello there. Do I get your company during my rotations this morning?" he asked with a wink, looking in my direction.

"If you're lucky," Joanna retorted from the bed, pausing to take another sip of apple juice.

Chris grinned, squeezing her foot through the sheets as he stopped at the base of the bed to lift the computer tablet mounted there. "Have you checked her vitals yet?" he asked.

"Not yet, I just got here."

"And I had a coughing fit to tell her good morning," Joanna said with a laugh, another shaky cough coming on the heels of that.

Chris rounded the bed to stand beside me, and we both glanced at the tablet screen. Joanna's vitals were about where they'd been for days now. She was eschewing most medications, and that was her choice. Seeing as she was pushing ninety-four years old now, I figured by the time you reach that age, you got to go however you chose. Joanna had been dealing with complications from Chronic Obstructive Pulmonary Disease. She was never a smoker, but her late husband had been.

"I'd ask if you wanted any medication for that cough, but I think I know the answer," Chris commented when she coughed again.

I took her paper cup from her and filled it with juice again. After a few shuddering breaths, she nodded. "Of course you know the answer. I don't like being sleepy."

"Are you up for breakfast this morning?" I asked.

"Send it up," she said with a wink.

"Gotcha. Well, I'm just here this morning, but you know how to buzz me if you need me," I said, as I adjusted the pillows behind her.

Chris tapped a few things on the tablet screen and went to refill her IV bag, as I headed out the door.

Chapter Nine

HOLLY

After leaving Joanna's room, I checked on another few patients before stopping at the nurse's station on this floor. The staff was thin this morning, just myself as supervisor and a few other nurses on this floor. Within another hour or two, more staff would start to filter in.

Chris rounded the circular nurse's station, coming to lean against the counter behind it. "What's up?" he asked, crossing his arms and glancing at me

Clicking into the computer system where all of our client records were managed, I tapped a few keys and quickly entered the update for my rounds this morning. Glancing up, I shrugged. "Not much. It's quiet this morning, which I don't mind. How are things with you?"

Chris flashed a grin. "Pretty good, actually. Aaron and I finally set a wedding date," he said, referring to his long-term boyfriend.

"Oh, that's awesome! So, when is it and am I going to be invited?"

Chris and Aaron had been together since college, over ten years now. He had been ecstatic when same-sex marriage was legalized in Alaska. They promptly got engaged, but that had been a full year ago. Of late, Chris has been complaining about settling on a wedding date.

"Of course you're invited! The wedding will be next summer. We might have it in Diamond Creek. It's one of our favorite places to visit for weekends, especially in the summer. I mean, you know Aaron is such a freaking man, Mister Fisher-hunter guy. He loves that outdoor stuff."

"And you fucking love that about him," I said with a laugh. Sobering, I reached out to catch his hand and give it a quick squeeze. "I'm seriously happy for you."

"I know you are. Speaking of love lives, how's yours?" he asked pointedly.

Chris had been on my case lately to actually do something about the fact that I want a chance at something serious. Like all the rest of my friends, he was blessedly oblivious to my virgin state. I couldn't help but wonder if that was interfering with everything for me.

I eyed him for a moment, deciding he might be my best bet for some advice. While we were close, he was a little outside the tight bubble of my childhood friends. He moved to Willow Brook after he graduated from nursing school and snagged a position supervising the non-emergency nursing staff. He was certainly friends with many of my friends. Yet, nosy as he was, he was a tad less opinionated about my life.

Steeling myself, I took a deep breath and blurted out the blunt truth. "I'm a virgin, and I think it's fucking with my head. Oh, and I still haven't gone on a date with Nate."

Beyond my friend Megan in Anchorage, Chris was actually the only person I had told about the catastrophic fundraiser last fall that was supposed to be fun. At my announcement, his eyes widened and his mouth dropped open. Catching himself, he snapped it shut. "Well, damn. It's not easy to surprise me."

I hurried to clarify. "Before you go making assumptions about it, it's kind of an accident. I haven't been saving myself. It's just that when everybody else was busy losing their virginity, Jake died in that car accident and it pretty much threw everything out of whack in my life. It had this weird side effect where everybody assumed I was heart-broken over the love of my life dying. But we weren't like that. Not like Ella and Caleb," I explained. Chris knew their whole glorious second chance romance and thought it was amazing. "Honestly, if he hadn't died, we probably would've broken up and stayed friends, and it would've been fine. Anyway, all the guys in town wouldn't even pay attention to me after the accident. It was so weird." I shook my head and groaned, burying my face in my hands.

When I looked up, Chris leaned over and gave me a quick hug. "It all kind of makes sense. Shit like that fucks with your social life and your sex life."

"Right," I muttered. "Since then, it's not like I haven't dated and experienced all kinds of foreplay. It's just that that whole sex thing never happened. I don't technically think I'm a virgin, by the way."

Chris burst out laughing and shook his head slowly. "I technically think you are."

"I don't think so. I have vibrators," I offered.

By the time he stopped laughing, tears were rolling down his cheeks. I was relieved it was quiet at the hospital this morning because we hadn't been interrupted, and it didn't look like we would be anytime soon. Nobody else was due for a shift in this unit for another half hour. Unless we got buzzed, we were in the clear.

"Great, I'm glad you have vibrators. I'm not a woman, but I still don't think that counts," he finally said.

I sighed, standing and striding to the back of the nurse's station where there was one of those convenient single serve coffee makers. "Coffee?" I called over my shoulder. "I need a cup to get through the rest of this conversation."

"Sure, I'll take the chocolate stuff."

I started his coffee, leaning my hips against the counter

while we waited. "I guess this is my long way of explaining where I'm at."

Chris's gaze sobered as he sank into the chair I had just vacated, propping his feet up on the counter and spinning to look at me with a push. "I don't think it should make a difference. If it's the right guy, well, I guess he should be excited. Like, that's a *thing* for straight men, right? You know, being a woman's first?"

I snorted as I checked the coffee, turning to take his cup out and handing it over with a small container of cream from a bowl beside the machine. "I don't know. I'm not a guy. You should know better than me."

"Okay, it's a thing. I'll just repeat what I said. I don't think it should be a big deal. Maybe you should just get it out of the way if you're worried about it," he replied as he took the cup of coffee from me.

"With who?" I countered, flinging my hands up and turning back to put in a single shot of dark brew. Hitting the button to start it, I listened to the hum of the machine as I faced Chris again.

He shrugged. "Well, if you think it's a barrier, then just get rid of it. It's not like you were saving it for someone special. On another note, you're telling me you still haven't made good on that expensive date Nate bought with you? It sounds like the guy did you a freaking favor."

The following day, I had actually gone back and talked with Ethan and Megan. They confirmed the other bids were definitely from people they didn't think I would have cared to be pushed into a date with. Megan had told me to get over myself, go on the date with Nate, and have a good time. Little did she know, we'd had a hot, crazy kiss in the dressing room after the fact.

"I know," I muttered. "Look, I need some serious guy advice. Because I don't know who else to talk to about this. Anybody I talk to is friends with both of us."

"And I'm not?" Chris countered, looking affronted.

"You are, but you're the least likely to be judgmental about it."

"Okay, so what's your question?"

"I might've left out a few details about me and Nate. We might have almost had sex twice now."

Chris leaned forward in his chair, slapping his palm on the counter. "Oh my God. What the hell? You are *seriously* holding out on me."

My face was on fire, and I turned away as I heard the coffee machine stop humming. Gathering myself, I poured a dash of cream in my coffee and took a gulp before I turned back to face the music.

"I don't know what to do," I said with a sigh, leaning my hips on the counter.

"Okay, I'll forget about how annoyed I am you haven't mentioned a thing about this to me. What do you want to do?"

I took a sip of my coffee and shrugged. "I dunno."

"Well, it sounds like you want to *do* Nate," he countered with a sly grin.

I giggled, my cheeks heating again. "Yeah, but you know Nate. He's all about no strings attached. The last thing I want is to be added to his 'list,' so to speak."

Chris eyed me, cocking his head to the side. "I think Nate likes you. And who cares if he's usually about no strings? He might be the perfect candidate for you to *technically* dump your virginity. You don't even have to tell him about your virginity. "Technically"—he paused, air quotes and all, and dragging out the technically a bit more than I appreciated—"you're not a virgin. Although, I bet he's hung and that might give it away."

I burst out laughing, guessing he was quite right in that regard. Although I hadn't ever seen the evidence with my own eyes, I had a good sense of just how well-endowed Nate was.

"Maybe you have a point. As far as not telling him though, I already blew that."

"You *told* him?" Chris asked, his eyes widening.

"Yes," I murmured. "It kind of slipped out because I was pissed off at him. It did get him to shut up though."

Chris threw his head back with a laugh. "Oh my God! I would've loved to have been there for that. Look, I don't know what to tell you, but there's no way to know in advance if anybody you're with is going to work out to be the one. You're not gonna know that. It seems like you and Nate might have a little bit of something to get out of your systems, so why not do something about it? Even though he keeps things casual, he's not an asshole and he doesn't really do the local dating thing. He sows his oats in the summer and then lays low in the winter. He's kind of like a bear in that regard."

I almost spit out my coffee at that. Nate didn't look like a bear, but thinking of him like that was too damn funny. At that moment, my pager went off, calling me down to the ED. I straightened, about to hurry away when I felt Chris's hand on my shoulder.

"What?" I asked, turning back as he stood from the chair.

"Never stop being awesome. That's one of my favorite things about you. You're kickass. Stop worrying about being a virgin and stop worrying about planning things out ahead. You're getting all up in your head and that's what's getting in your way." At that, he tugged me in for a quick hug and then spun me around before I hurried off.

Chapter Ten

NATE

I leaned back in my chair at Wildlands, scanning the room full of people. I wasn't here with friends tonight. I'd stopped by after a pretty bumpy flight in from a regularly scheduled delivery of mail and groceries to a nearby Alaska Native village. A storm had kicked up almost out of nowhere on my return.

Taking a pull on my beer, I attempted to get interested in a woman sitting at the corner of the bar. She had long dark hair and was tall and willowy. Objectively speaking, she was beautiful, and she wasn't local. I'd never seen her before and I heard from Mike the bartender that she was passing through to handle a supply delivery for the hospital.

No matter how long I looked at her, I felt nothing. In fact, the idea of trying to flirt with her left a bad taste in my mouth. It had nothing to do with her, and *everything* to do with Holly. It had been three full days since Holly dropped the little bomb about her virginity, and I'd barely been able to stop thinking about it. I had talked myself into this idea that, maybe, just maybe, I wanted something more than casual with Holly. She was *that* girl, the one I'd never been able to shake free from my thoughts. Finally, I thought I had a shot, and then she went and dropped that bit of info.

What the hell?

It didn't change the state of my desire for her, not one bit. Yet, it felt heavy now, weighted with a sense of meaning and depth that gave me pause.

I stood from my chair, threading my way through the clusters of people to the bar. I figured perhaps I just needed to get close enough to the woman there to remind my body that I could want someone other than Holly. Reaching the woman in question, I leaned my elbow on the bar and set my half-empty beer bottle down.

The woman glanced my way. She had beautiful blue eyes. Even though my gaze reflexively flicked down to notice she had generous breasts, there was absolutely no reaction from my body.

Even worse, my brain instantly conjured up an image of Holly, her long blonde hair up in its usual messy bun or slap-dash ponytail, her wide brown eyes, and her compact, curvy build. Now *that* vision was something my body could latch onto, my cock stirring at nothing more than the thought of Holly.

I told myself I just needed to trigger my muscle memory. I just needed to go through the motions of flirting and teasing with this woman and then my body would remember what I wanted and, more importantly, forget Holly.

I was experiencing a definite first. I couldn't even come up with a quick way to say hello. Even when I wasn't trying to flirt or pick someone up, I was always fast with a quip with any man, woman, or inanimate object. I smiled blandly at her, turning away when the bartender asked me a question.

"You need another one?" Mike asked, eyeing my beer.

"No thanks. I gotta go."

I hadn't even finished my beer, and I left, annoyed, rest-less, and frustrated as hell with my state of mind. I didn't realize what I was doing until I turned my truck out of the parking lot in the direction opposite my place. Holly lived a mere block or two down the road from Wildlands.

I knew what I wanted with Holly. I just didn't quite know how to go about getting it. I figured we could start by throwing a match and a splash of gasoline on the fire burning between us.

To my knowledge, I hadn't had sex with a virgin before. When I was in high school, the first girl I'd ever been with had already taken care of that. We had simply had fun together. We dated for a few months after her ex-boyfriend, who she adored, had screwed around on her. We were still friends to this day, although she didn't live in Willow Brook anymore. She lived in Anchorage and was happily married with a few kids.

After that, well, life just kept going. Casual was the name of the game, but that wasn't what I wanted with Holly. Niggling in the back of my mind was the thought that she was still hung up on Jake. I cut the engine on my truck beside her car in the small parking lot behind the building. I'd been here before, but never alone. Here and there, she would have friends over, but I was almost always with Alex. I looked up to the back window to see the light glowing.

What I wanted — or rather, *who* I wanted — overrode every ounce of common sense I had. I'd like to chalk it up to being drunk and stupid, but I'd only had maybe half a beer. Before I knew it, I was standing at her kitchen door and raising my hand to knock sharply three times.

The door swung open, and Holly stood there. The second I laid eyes on her, lust bolted through me, hard and fast. Her hair was up in a ponytail with loose tendrils escaping and falling around her face. Her brown eyes widened when she saw me, and a flush crested on her cheeks. She wore a V-neck cotton T-shirt, the fabric worn and thin. My eyes immediately noticed she wasn't wearing a bra. Her full breasts stretched the T-shirt, her nipples visible in tight little peaks through the fabric. Below that, she wore a pair of swingy cotton pants that rested low on her hips, offering me a glimpse of skin between where her shirt ended and the waistband began. Her feet were bare and her toenails painted bright blue.

We must've stood there a few beats too long because I saw her shiver. Only then did it occur to me it was freezing outside. "Mind if I come in?" I asked.

She shook her head and stepped back. "Might as well, it's freezing out there." Stepping back, she let me pass, quickly closing the door behind me. "What the hell are you doing here? It's almost ten o'clock."

I took a moment, gathering my thoughts, as my eyes coasted over her small apartment. It was one large room with the kitchen to the side where I had entered, a small island separating it from the living room, which had a high ceiling and windows that looked out over Main Street, currently cast in darkness. A sectional couch faced the windows on one side and the wall on the other where a television was mounted. Aside from a coffee table and two end tables, that was the extent of her furnishings.

Just now, it occurred to me I hadn't actually ever been in her bedroom. I could see through the open door to a queen-size bed piled high with pillows and a fluffy, navy down quilt.

"Well?" Holly asked.

My eyes made their way back to her. I didn't have any sensible reason for showing up at her apartment unannounced at this hour. Before any thoughts could form in my brain, I stepped to her, and turned. She retreated slightly, leaning against the wall right beside the door. She opened her mouth, I presumed to argue with me about something.

"I have an idea," I said quickly.

She looked annoyed. Her cheeks were flushed, and I could see the rapid flutter of her pulse along the side of her neck. I could also feel the tight little points of her nipples pressing against my chest as her breath came in sharp little pants. I knew what it felt like to have her come all over my fingers, now I wanted to feel her come all over my cock and my mouth.

"What?" she countered.

"You said you weren't saving yourself, and that your virginity was a problem. Let's take care of it."

My brain was not functioning. At all. The moment my insane proposal flew out, a gear shifted.

What the hell are you doing?

What I want.

My retort was swift and true. I wanted Holly. Fiercely.

I could practically see the wheels turning in her brain, thoughts shifting wildly as she stared at me, her cheeks flushing a deeper shade of red. Her tongue darted out, swiping across her bottom lip and sending another hot jolt of lust through me. My cock was hard, so hard it ached. I knew she could feel it, pressing against her lower belly.

"You mean like a one-time thing?" she asked.

Something passed through the depths of her eyes, my heart giving a hard kick to my ribs in response. Holly didn't usually exude vulnerability. She was strong, sassy, and opinionated as hell. She was never one to back down. Yet, I sensed a glimmer of vulnerability in her, and it gave me pause.

While I knew she trusted me as a friend, she'd made it fairly clear she didn't trust me in this respect. I knew I had to show her she was wrong. I also knew there was no way I was going to sweet talk her into this, and had every intention of taking full advantage of the white-hot need that had caught fire between us.

She was quiet for a beat too long, and I sensed she was going to argue the point. "Maybe, maybe not. Let's see what happens," I finally replied.

Her breasts pressed against me when she took a deep breath. It was about all I could do not to rock my hips into her.

She surprised me next. "Okay," she said on a soft exhale.

Somehow, even though this was exactly what I wanted, I hadn't thought past this moment. Well, it was fair to say *thought* didn't have much to do with what was happening. Abruptly, I reminded myself she was a virgin. Much as I wanted to, I couldn't fuck her up against the wall. It didn't seem right.

Let me clarify. It seemed quite right, but I'd have to save that for another time. The vision of Holly's legs curled around me, bare naked and her skin flushed pink all over as I fucked her, was enough to bring me to my knees. But that was the kind of thing to save for after she wasn't a virgin.

I'd never been one of those men who thought too much about a woman's virginity. It wasn't like something I owned, or something to claim. I was realizing that perhaps I hadn't cared because I hadn't let myself care about any woman enough. Ever since Holly's little bombshell the other day, I'd been thinking that I couldn't fucking believe no other man had been lucky enough to have all of her.

Chapter Eleven

NATE

I didn't wait, lifting a hand and brushing a few loose tendrils of hair off her cheek before I leaned forward, speaking against her lips. "Okay then, let's do this," I murmured.

She immediately arched into me, sliding a hand around the nape of my neck and murmuring, "For God's sake, kiss me."

Leave it to Holly to take control of the situation.

No sense in arguing with her. Our mouths collided. I was coming to learn that one thing Holly and I did incredibly well together was kiss. Jesus fucking Christ, I could kiss her for days. She didn't hold back, her soft sensuous lips moving against mine, her tongue darting in to glide against mine.

I loved the sounds she made, little pants and moans, right into my mouth. I lost all sense of time. I didn't even know how fast it happened, but I was lifting her as her legs wrapped around my waist. I could feel the damp heat of her through her thin cotton pants and the denim of my jeans.

Through the haze, I reminded myself this wasn't just any woman. This was Holly, the woman I had fantasized about for years and told myself I couldn't have. And she was a virgin. I needed to get this right. Scrambling for purchase in my mind and latching onto what little control I had, I broke free from our kiss, gulping in a breath of air.

Holding her against me, I turned away from the wall. "Bedroom," I muttered.

She laughed, the husky sound sending a hot shot of blood to my groin. It would be a fucking miracle if I didn't come in my pants over this woman.

"What? Is this one of those things where you think you have to do this right? We almost fucked in an elevator. Not to mention, I don't think this virginity thing is going to be all that you think it is. It's not like nothing's ever happened, and I have plenty of vibrators."

Dear God. I might end up actually praying to maintain my restraint. The vision of Holly playing with herself nearly snapped what little control I had left. Like I said, it'd be a miracle if I didn't blow this before it came to prime time.

Angling in the direction of her bedroom, I held her high against me. "Shut up."

"Oh, like that's going to happen," she teased as I shouldered through the door into her bedroom.

On the heels of another giggle, she dipped her head and nipped at my neck. I hadn't been kidding myself, she was the opposite of passive. Hell, she climbed me like a damn tree in the dressing room after the fundraiser. Not to mention what happened in the elevator.

Yet, three days of mulling over the bombshell that she was a virgin, and I'd worked myself up into this idea where I needed to be gentle with her. Holly was having none of that. Another nip on my neck, and then when I paused at the foot of the bed, she nudged my shoulder. "Get on with it, would you?"

"For fuck's sake, Holly," I muttered.

I started to ease her down and she shimmied free of my hold, the subtle motion of her against my body tightening every fiber. Anticipation was thrumming through me and need shot like fire through my veins.

With one hand, she snagged the hem of her T-shirt and lifted it up and over her head in a swoop, where it drifted to the floor. I lost my breath. Literally. While I'd had plenty of fantasies about Holly's breasts, I hadn't seen them in their full glory until now.

I felt lightheaded for a beat. Her breasts were plump and round, the skin tight with her dusky pink nipples peaked for my touch. She caught my eyes, a slight grin curling the corner of her mouth.

"Oh, I see. What did you think? I was suddenly going to get shy? That's not how this came about. This"—she paused, circling her hand and rolling her eyes—"virginity thing. It's just, the right guy hasn't come along. But you have a point. I might as well get it out of the way. Then, it won't be a nuisance."

Although I could hardly think straight—hell, I didn't even know if I could be accused of having a thought—I experienced a pang at the way she spoke about her virginity. I sensed she'd cordoned me off, put me in a corner labeled "casual, friends with benefits." Considering that I practically specialized in casual, although I had avoided getting tangled up with friends, it wasn't like I could hold it against her, but still. Fortunately, she didn't let me dwell, stepping to me and swiftly shoving my jacket off my shoulders. "You have too many clothes on," she murmured.

She slid her hand up under my T-shirt, the feel of her palm sending streaks of fire over the surface of my skin. The tethers of my control were slipping, so I tightened my grip. Reaching behind my neck, I caught the collar of my shirt and tugged it over my head, flinging it to the side where it fell on the floor with hers. Yanking a condom out of my wallet, I tossed it on the nightstand by her bed as I kicked my jeans off.

When I looked back to Holly, she was shimmying out of

her cotton pants, kicking them free from her feet. Fuck me. For too long, she had been testing my restraint. I wasn't sure if this was some form of punishment at this point.

She stood before me, her breasts tempting me beyond belief. My eyes soaked up every detail—the dip at her waist, the soft curve of her belly, the flare of her hips—all of it combining to make me nearly crazy without even laying a finger on her.

Of course, to tempt me to the very edge of my restraint, she was wearing a scrap of navy blue silk for panties. She moved to hook her fingers on the edge of the silk, and I yanked on the reins of my control.

"No," I muttered, my word coming out a rough order.

Her wide brown eyes flicked to mine. "No?"

"Not yet."

Closing the distance between us, I almost groaned when I slid my hand into her hair and the other down her spine over the sweet curve of her ass. I'd felt Holly against me before, but there had always been at least a layer or two between us. When I felt her breasts against my chest, her bare skin soft and silky, it was like bolts of lightning zapping under my skin.

I needed her distracted, needed her as lost as I was. I claimed her lips, pouring the desire storming through me into her mouth. She fed the storm kiss for kiss, stroke for stroke, nip for nip. One hand mapped my chest with the other sliding down my spine, her nails scoring me lightly. I clung to some semblance of control if only because she was everything I wanted. *Finally.* Having her naked in my arms was a fantasy I'd had for so damn long, it was practically imprinted in my brain.

The relief of actually *feeling* her was immense. I tumbled us onto the bed, rolling to the side, finally giving in and breaking free of her lips to explore every inch of her delicious body. Her skin tasted sweet and salty. Cupping one of her breasts, I looked up when she arched into me, a soft moan escaping.

My fantasies about her had been poorly uninformed. I'd had a little more to hang onto the scaffolding of them since our recent close encounters. Yet, nothing could've prepared me for how exquisite it would feel to have her naked against me, with nothing but that tiny scrap of silk keeping me from all of her.

I brushed my thumb back and forth across the tight bead of her nipple before dipping my head to swirl my tongue around it, sucking it in and nipping lightly as she cried out. I dallied on the other breast, circling my finger in the moisture left behind from my tongue.

It was all a blur—her fingers buried in my hair on a rough gasp, my own ragged breathing, my cock so hard it ached, and need beating like a drum inside of me with every touch.

I blazed a trail over the soft curve of her belly, savoring the give of her skin as I gripped her hip and leaned back. When I dragged my fingers between her thighs, the silk was drenched. I knew what she felt like, the slick feel of her on my fingers. I couldn't fucking wait to be buried deep inside of her.

But first, I needed to make her lose her mind.

Teasing my fingers over the silk, I watched her face. Her cheeks were flushed, her entire body glistening with a sheen of sweat. The soft glow of a lamp in the corner was the only light in the room, casting her in a haze of gold.

"Nate," she gasped, her hips flexing into my touch.

I couldn't help the roll of satisfaction at the knowledge she wanted me this much.

"What?" I murmured in reply.

Her hair was a tangled mess on the pillows around her. She lifted her head, one elbow sliding back as she propped herself up. My cock throbbed. She was fucking glorious, her nipples all but begging for me to suck and lick them again.

As I waited, her eyes narrowed. Oh good, I loved Holly angry.

"Get on with it," she ordered.

She shifted, reaching for me. "Not so fast," I said, catching her hand in my free one just as I pushed that silk out of the way and buried my fingers in her channel. She was hot and wet. Whatever she meant to say next blended into a rough cry as she fell back against the pillows, her hips bucking into me.

There was no such thing as finesse when it came to Holly and me. It was like two sparks colliding and feeding the flames, setting off more and more fires everywhere we touched.

I shifted down, and pushed her knee to the side. Leaning forward, I dragged my tongue through her folds. Her channel clenched, squeezing my fingers. Needing her panties out of the way, I drew back just long enough to yank them down her legs and fling them across the room. Then, I buried my face between her thighs, licking, sucking, stroking, all the while teasing her with my fingers as she moaned and her hips rocked into me.

I felt the ripples of her climax begin, her sex clenching tighter before she cried out. My name was a rough shout as she came in a noisy burst. I'd meant to take it slow, but then that would've required some sort of control. With a yank and a kick, my briefs fell to the floor at the foot of the bed. I was mapping my way back up her body with my lips and tongue. I was after only one thing, the feel of her around me as I finally, fucking finally, buried myself inside this woman who had tortured my fantasies for years.

My hips settled in the cradle of hers, the slick, wet heat of her teasing me as I rocked my hips against her once, my cock sliding easily through her slippery folds. Reality suddenly hit me like a slap. I was so lost in the tornado of need whipping inside me that I almost forgot a condom.

Rolling away quickly, or rather trying to, I muttered, "Condom."

Holly had hooked her legs around my hips and held me fast. She was a small woman, at least on the height side, but she was strong. When I looked down, she met my gaze, her eyes wide and dark.

"Holly?"

She gave her head a shake and then eased her grip on my hips. I moved fast, reaching for the condom on her night-stand and getting it on in no time. When I settled back over her, about lost at the feel of her against me, I forcefully punched through the haze of desire in my mind. "Are you sure about this?"

She giggled, the sound making my heart squeeze. "I think it's a little late to back out now, don't you?"

This was heavy, heavier than I had expected. All fantasies aside, this was Holly, a woman I'd known for as long as I could remember. I was about to be the first man who had ever been inside of her like this. It might take every ounce of willpower I had, but if she changed her mind, I would respect it.

Chapter Twelve

HOLLY

Nate's dark gaze held mine, the look there so intense, it took my breath away. I could feel his cock, long, hard, and thick, resting against me. I'd just had an explosive orgasm, courtesy of his fingers and mouth. I should've been sated, and I wasn't even close.

And now, *now*, he wanted to know if I wanted to back out. If I had any sense, we wouldn't be bare ass naked in my bedroom, seconds away from me making what would probably be an epically bad mistake.

None of that figured into this moment. All that mattered was the drumbeat of my heart, need mingling with emotion and spinning into a storm inside, and the near desperate ache to feel him inside of me.

"I'm sure," I said.

My hips arched reflexively, the feel of him sliding over my swollen clit sending a hot little jolt of pleasure through me. I wanted more. Finally, *finally*, he gave it to me. When he drew back, I felt the tip of his cock at my entrance. All teasing aside about technicalities, for a moment, I experienced a flash of anxiety.

And then he was sliding inside, an incrementally slow, deep stroke. I sensed him hanging onto his control. He was taut as a bow, every hard inch of him even harder as he slowly filled me. There was a subtle pinch and burn, but it wasn't awful. Perhaps I'd been right that my vibrators had helped.

His voice was almost slurred when he spoke. "Holly, are you okay?"

"Mmm-hmm," I managed, my heart beating so hard and fast it thundered through my body.

My hips rocked into him again, another subtle burn stinging me. But it felt good, the feel of him stretching and filling me felt better than I could've imagined. I knew I'd been missing out, I guess I just hadn't realized how much.

Nate drew back slowly and then sank inside again. Again, I sensed him trying to measure this, trying to manage it. Restless with a burning, yearning need driving me, I arched into him, my hips rising to meet every stroke. I was too caught up in slick sensation, too tied up to let this be drawn out, to let this be slow.

Curling my legs around his hips, I slid my hand down his spine. "Don't make me wait," I murmured.

Our gazes collided, his dark and intent. Something flickered there that reached straight into my heart, hooking deeply. I felt as if I were spinning. With every stroke of him inside me, his skin against mine, his hard muscled body surrounding me, I was caught in a web of desire and intimacy.

"I'm not rushing just because you say so," he said, his gruff voice whispering against my lips.

It was true that I hadn't been saving myself, yet I couldn't have been prepared for this. I felt as if I'd be ruined forever. Having this with Nate being my first experience, I was tossed asunder on the waves of emotion and desire crashing against the rocks.

Everything blurred. With his hips rocking into mine, he

took complete control, not that I could've taken it back. It was a slow-motion dance of madness with his hard muscled body against mine, and every surge of his cock into the clenching walls of my sex. Slick and wet, the pull and glide of him pushed me higher and higher, pressure gathering in my core.

All the while, his eyes were on me and I couldn't look away. Pleasure scattered through me and sparks caught hold, fire flashing through me. He reached between us, shifting up slightly with another slow drive into me. With the press of his thumb over my clit, the pressure spun loose, snapping with such force that I cried out.

He kept moving and my orgasm just kept going and going and going, clenching tightly down around his cock. I was spent from the force of it when it finally started to subside. I felt him go taut with a rough shout. On the heels of that, he collapsed against me, rolling us so he was on his back as I rested, limp and sated against his chest.

I was boneless, spinning in the currents. Nate murmured something and brushed my damp hair back away from my face.

"Are you okay?"

That simple question, which I presumed was tied to his concern that somehow this had hurt me. Oh, there had been a bit of a burn and a stretch, definitely more than anything I had experienced before, yet somehow, it chafed at me to have him ask.

Probably because I felt too vulnerable, too exposed— caught in an undercurrent of desire and intimacy far more intense than anything I had experienced before. I couldn't have said why things had never gone further with other men, not when I wasn't holding back on purpose. But this—the way I felt with Nate—was so much more than I had expected.

Emotions slammed through me, and I couldn't quite speak. Unable to look away from his dark chocolate gaze, I managed to nod. I was barely there mentally, still awash in sensation, little shudders rippling through my body, pleasure pinging in tiny aftershocks.

Our breath slowed in unison, and I managed to finally get enough oxygen to think. With his arm around my back, one palm cupping my bottom and the other sifting through my hair, I told myself I needed to move. But I didn't want to.

This all felt too good. I hadn't expected losing my virginity to carry this much weight. I wanted to wrap myself in Nate and ignore the world. But I couldn't. I needed to keep the boundaries clear, for myself as much as for him.

Steeling myself, I lifted my head, resting my chin on my hand. Nate's eyes opened. I would've given just about anything to know what he was thinking. As long as I had known him, he'd never been that easy to read. At least, not beyond what he showed the world. There was Nate the tease, the flirt who everybody knew. Just now, though, looking into his gaze, I had no idea what he was thinking. His hand stilled for a moment in my hair and then he lifted it, brushing another tangled lock off my forehead.

This was all too much, too much of what I wanted. I forced myself to move. Rising up, I looked down, realizing I was straddling him. When my hips shifted, I felt his cock swell inside of me. His mouth kicked up at the corner. "Don't do that," he murmured.

I hadn't meant to, I wasn't purposefully teasing, but my hips moved on their own, rocking slightly. No matter what I told myself, my body knew what I wanted, or rather *who*— Nate. It didn't seem to matter that he'd just sent me flying not once, but twice.

"You figuring out how to chase me out?" he asked.

He promptly pissed me off. Not that I was about to let him know. It chafed to realize how well and how easily he could read me. Because he was right. The moment the wheels in my brain had started to spin, I was wondering how to gracefully chase him out of my apartment.

Not because I actually wanted to. No, rather because I wanted him to stay. Far too much. And it scared the hell out of me.

Mustering my composure, I rolled my eyes. "No, I wasn't going to chase you out."

If he knew I was lying, he let it slide. A sense of self-consciousness rose within. I hadn't wanted my virginity to be a thing. Yet, here I was, with that burden finally gone, and I was with Nate. I'd known him forever, and he was one of the very few people who knew that little secret.

I didn't know how to be nonchalant about untangling myself from him. He saved me from having to sort that one out. Whether it was because he sensed my uncertainty, or simply convenient timing, he shifted slightly, lifting me as he slid out. For a flash, I felt bereft, instantly missing the point of joining.

He rolled slightly, slipping out from underneath me and standing. When I looked up at him in the dim light, my breath caught. It wasn't as if I hadn't seen Nate shirtless before. He was my twin brother's best friend, after all. He'd spent many a night at our house in high school, both of them lounging around in sweatpants and no shirts at least half the time.

But that was before the switch had been flipped in my body. Now, I couldn't look at him and not feel an answering ping inside my own body. He held his hand out. I must've stared at him blankly because his mouth curled up in that one corner.

"Shower," he said, as if that made perfect sense.

I wasn't thinking very much just now. It was easier not to. Placing my hand in his, there was a little jolt of heat, a *zing* of electricity at the point of contact. He curled his hand around mine, giving a gentle tug, his grip warm and strong.

Chapter Thirteen

HOLLY

I came awake when I heard a soft rustling in the bedroom. I must've made a sound, because I heard Nate's voice. Stepping to the side of the bed, he leaned over, his lips dusting across mine. Instantly, I wanted to tug him to me and tumble into the very same madness I'd lost myself in last night.

"Gotta go," he said, his voice a gruff whisper.

I'd completely and utterly failed in my intent to not fall asleep with him last night. After he challenged me by expecting me to chase him off, I couldn't bring myself to do it. I didn't want to prove him right. Even more, I didn't want him to leave.

I vaguely remembered that he had mentioned he had to leave early this morning to fly a group of backcountry skiers out to a lodge. He wouldn't be returning for three days.

"Oh, right," I replied, shifting up in bed. The covers rumpled around my waist as I slid up on the pillows. Brushing my tangled hair back from my face, I looked up at him. "Do you need some coffee?"

"You don't need to get up on my account, and you need to cover up," he said with a low chuckle.

With the light from the bathroom cast across the room, I saw his eyes flick down to my bare breasts. My nipples tightened in response. Before I could form a thought, he dipped his head and caught one of my nipples in his lips with a quick swirl of his tongue and a light graze of his teeth. Just like that, my sex clenched, an ache building between my thighs.

He stepped back swiftly. Restless, I kicked the sheets off and grabbed my robe draped on a chair beside the bed. I walked past him. "I get up early anyway. I have to be at the hospital in two hours. I'll make you coffee before you go. Do you have time?" I called over my shoulder as I strode quickly out of the bedroom into the kitchen and flicked on a light.

It was six thirty a.m. The sun would rise in roughly an hour and a half or so.

"I have time. You don't..." His words trailed off when I glanced back at him and shook my head as I tightened the sash on my robe.

I needed something to do. I sure as hell didn't want to lie in bed lusting after Nate. He chuckled as he slipped onto a stool by the counter. "If you insist. I've got about a half hour."

"Perfect. Enough time for me to make coffee and some food for you."

"You don't..." He laughed this time when I sent a pointed glare in his direction.

"You need breakfast. Janet's scones are delicious, but she doesn't start serving actual breakfast for another hour. I'll have an egg sandwich ready for you inside of ten minutes."

I started the coffee quickly, not wanting to dwell on the fact that I happened to know Nate loved egg sandwiches. He'd always asked my mother to make them whenever he spent the night with my brother when we were growing up. After I started the coffee, I pulled out the bread and cracked the eggs, pouring them into a small pan. I met my self-imposed ten-minute deadline with a minute to spare.

After sliding his coffee across the counter, I flipped his sandwich onto a plate with a spatula and handed it over. "Oh wait, hot sauce," I said. Spinning back, I reached into my cabinet and pulled out his favorite hot sauce. Lifting the top slice of bread, I sprinkled a few drops on the eggs.

He took a sip of his coffee and let out a sigh. "This is perfect."

I poured my own cup of coffee and hooked my foot around a stool to the side of the counter. Tugging it closer, I shimmied my hips on it and sipped my coffee while he ate.

I didn't quite know what to think about any of this. Last night had been... well, it had been *far* more than I had expected. Losing my virginity itself wasn't what had struck me at my core. Rather, it was the unexpected intimacy. Somehow, I doubted that feeling was simply lust, no matter how much I wanted to talk myself into the idea that it was.

Nate ate quietly, his eyes occasionally flicking to me. Otherwise, we sat in companionable silence. It wasn't as if I hadn't had breakfast with Nate before. In fact, I had many times. Alex was a late morning sleeper, in contrast to Nate and me. My mother used to make us breakfast whenever Nate spent the night, and Alex would usually come straggling in much later.

This brief, mundane interaction felt both familiar and entirely new. The factor thrown into the mix that changed the dynamics was the fact that I'd now been more intimate with Nate than any man before. Restless, I took a gulp of my coffee and stood from the counter, again tightening my robe. I was nervous, and I knew it.

Busying myself, I put the single pan I had used to make his egg sandwich in the sink and quickly washed it, also taking a moment to top off my coffee. When I turned back, I leaned my hips on the counter, gripping my coffee in one hand and curling the other around the ledge.

My eyes soaked up the sight of Nate. With his hair damp
from the shower, he was so damn handsome. He had short,
straight brown hair that fell in a shaggy cut around his ears
and over his forehead. I wanted to step to him and run my
fingers through it, and lose myself in his mouth again. He
had full, sensual lips. His features were on the sharp side
with distinct brows and angled cheekbones, the contrast
making his lips all the more decadent.

My pulse lunged the moment he pushed his plate away
and looked up. Oh geez. There'd been a reason I'd been
doing my damnedest to avoid close encounters with Nate.
My body went haywire every time I got close to him.

Now that I knew with every inch of my body what it felt
like to have him tangled up with me, buried to the hilt inside
of me, it was worse, definitely worse.

"Thanks," he said. "That was delicious." His eyes flicked
above my head to the clock above the stove. "I've gotta get
going. Need to make it to the hangar in time to get everything ready for the flight."

He stood, rounding the counter and quickly draining his
coffee before setting his mug and plate in the sink. I kept
telling my body to move, but I stayed right where I was. The
urge to be close to him overrode every ounce of common
sense. But then lately, my common sense had gone running
when it came to Nate. I was gripping my coffee mug as if my
life depended on it. Perhaps, if I held on tight enough, I
would be able to resist the urge to touch him.

He wore a faded pair of jeans that caressed his muscled
legs, with a white T-shirt and a worn, blue flannel shirt
hanging open. His layers weren't doing a damn thing to hide
his muscled chest and how well he filled out his clothes. I'd
seen him dressed like this far more times than I could count,
and yet my eyes soaked up the sight of him greedily,
hungering to touch him.

Now came the really awkward part. He would leave, and
maybe, just maybe, I could get my sanity back. Nate, once

again, blew my expectations out of the water. He rested a hand on either side of me on the counter, caging me in between his arms, a gleam in his eyes when he met my gaze.

"So."

"So, what?" I countered, trying to ignore the way my pulse took off at a gallop the moment he got this close to me.

"I'm surprised you didn't chase me out this morning," he murmured, that teasing, taunting look in his eyes amping me up.

I felt my cheeks heat and ignored it, willing my body to stand down. It ignored me entirely, my pulse galloping even faster and heat blooming from my core outward.

"I wasn't going to chase you out," I finally retorted, hating how easily he got under my skin.

"What now?" he asked, moving right along.

Now *that* was a question that had been spinning through my thoughts ever since I'd woken up and my brain had kicked into gear.

I needed to play this casual, for myself as much for him. I already knew I had tumbled into the danger zone when it came to Nate. I knew him too well, and I knew he didn't do serious, so I couldn't hope for anything more. But I wasn't about to let him see my vulnerability.

"I think now you go to work. I'm sure I'll see you around when you get back."

Nate's eyes narrowed, the teasing glint fading quickly. Good. I could deal with him being annoyed with me. To my chagrin, he didn't even argue the point.

In a hot second, his lips were on mine, his tongue sweeping into my mouth as I gasped. In all of two seconds, he crowded against me, pulling me close, his hand sliding down my spine to cup my ass as he rocked his arousal into me.

It was over before I could even form a thought. Then, he was stepping back, his gaze dark. At the look in his eyes, my lower belly clenched, and I became acutely aware of the slick heat of my desire between my thighs.

"Oh, you'll see me when I get back. This isn't close to over," he said. At that, he spun on his heel and strolled out, grabbing his jacket off the hook by the door and leaving with a wink and a grin.

The moment the door clicked shut behind him, I waited, listening to hear his footsteps treading down the stairs outside. With my heart thundering, I was hot, so hot and bothered, it made me angry.

As soon as I heard his engine start in the darkness, I hurried over and locked the door behind him, as if that would shield me from my own reaction to him.

Moments later, I was in the shower, the hot water cascading down around me, my mind replaying everything that happened last night. We had only had actual sex once. But that hadn't stopped me from waking him again during the night. When I had shifted against him, he murmured my name. Next thing I knew, his hands were mapping my body, and he buried his face between my legs and sent me flying again before rising above me, fisting his cock as he came all over my belly.

I blushed just thinking about it, and found myself stepping out of the shower and hunting down my favorite vibrator to bring myself to a fierce and almost instantaneous climax.

I was in trouble, deep trouble.

Chapter Fourteen

NATE

Angling the plane in the sky, I looked ahead out over the mountain range spread before us. Alaska was stunning in any season, but winter illuminated its raw beauty. Snow-capped mountains rose in the distance, bright and almost blinding white against the blue sky. The low rumble of the plane's engine made chatter largely impractical while flying. With my headphones on, I could hear occasional comments from the group I was flying, but was otherwise left to my own devices.

For the most part, I preferred it that way. I was by no means a shy guy. I freely admitted to being a tease and flirt, yet I loved flying for the sense of peace it brought me. The focus of flying above the sheer beauty of Alaska quieted me. It was one of the reasons I'd fallen in love with flying. My father had gotten his private pilot's license while he was working as an engineer on the Alaskan Pipeline back during its construction. I'd loved going on short flights with him when I was a kid when he took me out in his friend's plane.

The group I was ferrying today was going out to a

remote lodge for some backcountry skiing. They were what
I considered hardcore wilderness tourists around here. They
tended to take themselves far more seriously than most
Alaskans would. When you lived in Alaska, the wilderness
was your backyard with a few exceptions, such as the urban
areas of Anchorage, Fairbanks, and Juneau. Even then, the
streets had moose meandering along them and the wilderness was minutes away.

I didn't feel the need to fly out into the middle of
freakin' nowhere to do some backcountry skiing, but adventurers like this wanted to be able to mark it off on their
imaginary bucket list. I didn't mean to sound insulting, but I
suppose I didn't quite understand why they didn't just live
somewhere where the wilderness could be part of their
daily life.

I wasn't complaining, though. Trips like this were my
bread and butter. My flight schedule was varied with scheduled trips such as this, regular flights where I transported
mail, supplies, and passengers out to the array of rural
villages scattered across the Alaskan landscape, and then my
work for hotshot firefighting crews during the summers. I'd
make more this weekend than I would for several of the
other jobs. People paid a high price to get themselves out
exactly where they wanted to be.

Sometimes I returned home in between flights. This trip
was just enough of a distance that I was hunkering down at
the lodge for the long weekend before I flew the group back
to civilization.

The peace I sought from flying was a bit challenging to
come by today. Holly filled every corner of my thoughts.
Last night had been... I didn't have words to describe it.
There was fantasy, and then there was what happened when
reality trumped fantasy. I'd had a tease of Holly before last
night and knew the chemistry that caught fire between us
was damn near close to an inferno. Yet, actually getting skin-

to-skin with her and burying myself inside of her, well, it was safe to say she had permanently ruined me for any other woman. *Ever*.

I shoved my thoughts away from her when a glint of light reflected in the distance. There was a lake nestled in a valley up ahead where a high-end ski lodge was situated. The term "ski lodge" was used loosely here. By no means was this a place where they had chairlifts that carried skiers up a mountainside to ski down. Beyond the lodge itself, there was nothing here aside from wilderness, as far as the eye could see. The lodge was a high-end tricked out wilderness lodge with a few groomed cross-country ski trails nearby, and then miles upon miles of snow and mountains for free skiing.

I'd be landing my plane on the frozen lake. It served as a runway during the winter and summer. In the summer, I used my float plane, while in the winter, the snow-covered lake made for a smooth landing. I called in to report my status to air traffic control and then shifted the microphone away from my mouth to let the group know we'd be landing within a few minutes.

We were in my eight-seater plane, the largest one I flew. It was filled to capacity with this group—three couples and a friend. The friend in question happened to be a woman who had already tried to flirt with me. Under any other circumstances, I would have been happy to play along. She was gorgeous and funny. But if I thought I'd been out of whack after my kiss with Holly last October at the fundraiser, I was fucking screwed now.

Within minutes, I was easing the plane down on the icy lake, the snow blowing up around us as I landed. The weather had been near perfect today. On clear days, the wind could kick up. Today, we'd been blessed with a clear sky and almost no wind, which was a damn miracle in the winter in Alaska. Once we were on the ground—or the icy lake, rather —I helped everybody unload, and drove the plane over to the dock. The group began trekking through the snow to the lodge as I remained behind to tie down the plane.

My friend, Dave, waved from the entrance. Cupping my hands around my mouth, I called, "I'll be up in a bit, just taking care of the plane."

Dave and his wife, Nancy, owned this lodge and kept it in immaculate condition in the winter. Despite the isolation, they were never short on company. They had groups coming almost every weekend throughout the winter. The lodge ran on solar and wind power, and they had the water set up to recycle. The apocalypse could come, or whatever dystopia you wanted to imagine, and they would probably carry on just fine. They knew how to hunt, fish, and take care of themselves far better than most.

They even had a true-blue root cellar that they kept stocked to make it through the winter without any worry. Come summer, they had this huge lake for fishing, and hunting galore in the nearby areas. Dave and Nancy loved it out here and only flew into civilization, as they put it, two or three times a year for the holidays to visit family and take care of shopping. With satellite television and phone, they were good to go.

After I got the plane situated, I snagged my backpack and headed into the lodge. Normally, I looked forward to weekends like this. I could be lazy, watch television, eat good food, and lounge around. It was a genuine break from the world.

Yet, this time felt different. The days ahead—all two of them after today—stretched before me. I hadn't wanted to leave Holly this morning. I'd sensed the gears in her brain shifting as she tried to sort out just what I wanted. I knew we had chemistry. Hell, I didn't think there was any way she could deny that at this point. I also knew she wanted something serious. That was the part where I wasn't sure what she wanted with me. I had been her brother's friend since we were kids, and I knew that was how she had me categorized.

I kicked those thoughts to the curb as I crested the landing on the stairs to the backcountry luxury lodge.

"Hey, hey," Dave called as I closed the door behind me, knocking the snow off my boots in the entryway.

"Hey man," I replied. Leaning over, I quickly unlaced my boots and kicked them off. I left them over a narrow grate that ran along the outer wall where the snow could melt into a drain underneath. Boots, jackets, and other gear filled the entryway.

Slinging my backpack over my shoulder, I strolled into the main room to meet Dave. He pulled me close for a back-slapping hug and stepped back. The group I just delivered had already scattered to their rooms, I presumed.

"Which corner did you reserve for me?" I asked with a grin.

Dave chuckled. "I've only got one room left, man. It's down at the end of the hall upstairs. You've been in that one before, so you know where it is."

"Yup, know right where that is. You must have another group flying in then." I had only delivered seven guests and knew the lodge housed up to twenty.

"Oh yeah, got a group coming in from Fairbanks. They'll be here in about an hour."

"All right then, I'll go drop my stuff off. Nancy around?" I asked.

"Of course. She's in the kitchen. Meet us down there when you want. Sounds like your group is going to head out for a ski this afternoon, so unless you're going..." Dave let his words trail off with an arch of his brow.

Shaking my head, I chuckled. "I don't need to ski. I'm all set. I'm planning to be lazy this weekend." With a wave, I turned as Dave's laugh followed me out.

This lodge was beautiful. It was a two-story classic style timber frame lodge. Through the double-door entrance, which faced the lake, there was a large tiled foyer with rows of hooks for jackets and gear, and a narrow grate running along the entire wall for snow to melt without puddling on the floor.

A high ceiling with exposed beams opened up beyond the foyer to a large main room. Here, there were several areas for seating with sectionals and televisions on opposite sides of the rooms, views out the windows, and a central area with chairs, a game table, and small tables scattered around. Beyond that, to the back were two large dining tables, along with a smaller one by the wall. That allowed for big groups, or a more intimate setting if the lodge wasn't full. A door behind that led to a kitchen where Nancy, Dave's wife, did all of the cooking with occasional help when they had large groups. With twenty people here this weekend, I imagined she had called in some of her help.

Dave had grown up in the Willow Brook area, and Nancy was from Fairbanks. They met in college. They worked their tails off to buy this chunk of land and invest the money needed to have this place running the way it did. They made a pretty penny hosting wilderness tourists and adventurers. The lodge wasn't always full in the winter, but they were booked solid from late spring through autumn.

Rounding the base of the staircase off to one side of the main room, I jogged up the stairs. The upstairs was comprised of a long hallway, with bedrooms and suites flanking it on either side. Nancy and Dave had their own private quarters downstairs off the kitchen, with a private living room and master bedroom and bath. That way, they could get a little privacy when they needed it.

I'd known Dave for years. He'd been a few years ahead of me in high school and still came to Willow Brook for visits occasionally. The bedroom Dave had pointed me toward was right by the stairway. It was the smallest room in the lodge. Every room had a private bath, though, and there were a few suites for families or couples.

The bedrooms were open and airy with high ceilings,

exposed beams, and bright white walls to pull in all the light they could. There wasn't a single window in the lodge that didn't have a view of the mountains and wilderness. Although my room might have been the smallest, it was still luxurious and looked out over the lake. After dropping my bag and tossing my toiletries in the bathroom, I changed out of my heavier outdoor clothing and into a pair of comfortable jeans and a T-shirt.

Making my way back downstairs, I headed toward the kitchen. As I passed through the living room area, I saw the group I had just delivered tugging on their ski gear in the entryway. When I walked into the kitchen, Nancy looked up from where she was busy at a big worktable that ran through the center of the room.

"Nate!" she called with a wide grin. Her brown hair was pulled up into a ponytail and her blue eyes were bright with her smile. She set down whatever she was doing and wiped her hands on her apron as she rounded the table to give me a hug. "We haven't seen you in months."

"It's winter," I said with a shrug. "I don't get up here as often."

"I know. You could always come up just for a weekend if you want," she said as she returned to her task of chopping vegetables.

Dave stepped out of the door to the back that led to their quarters. "That's what he's doing this weekend. Why would he do it for free?" Dave asked with a chuckle, running a hand through his dark blond hair. "Coffee?" Dave paused beside the coffeemaker on the counter behind where Nancy was working, looking my way.

"I'd love some."

Dave filled two mugs and rounded the table, gesturing for me to sit beside him on one of several stools there.

After a welcome sip of coffee, my mind instantly spun back to this morning when Holly had insisted on making me

coffee and breakfast. My heart gave a hard thump, and I
forcefully pushed her out of my thoughts. I did *not* need to
spend the weekend dwelling on Holly, although I was confi-
dent that was what I'd be doing anyway.

"So, how's it going?" Nancy asked as she pulled out a bag
of onions from under the table.

"Busy, but then that's life, right?"

"So it is. Life still treating you right?" Dave asked in
return.

"Oh yeah. Nothing new, really."

Nancy looked up with a wicked grin. "Is this one of your
weekends where you have a fling?"

I shook my head. "Uh, no. Definitely not in the cards."

"Hmm. Well, that Gina woman was asking if you were
single," she said, referring to the only passenger who wasn't
paired up.

I almost choked on my coffee. She'd given off that
curious vibe, but I'd have expected her to play it a little
slower than that. Normally, I would find this amusing, but
just now, I didn't. I shrugged. "I'm just here to relax this
weekend, Nancy."

Dave took a swallow of his coffee and rolled his eyes.
"Well, not that you haven't done that before, but that'll be a
first when you have someone interested. You still the king of
casual?"

With Dave and Nancy paired up in college and married
for a good five years now, they weren't shy about teasing me
for playing the field. Normally, I took it in stride. Yet, right
now, it rankled a bit. Because this—this perception—was
precisely why I sensed Holly wasn't inclined to take me
seriously.

For about the thousandth time, I mentally kicked myself
for my brief freeze last year after our first kiss at that party.
In all honesty, I panicked. I'd written off any shot with her
for so long that it had startled me to see and feel her
responding desire. At the time, I'd wanted her fiercely. I'd

been relegated to the friend corner in her mind for as long as I'd known and hadn't expected anything else.

Truth be told, I also hadn't been ready. I wasn't about to get into all that with Nancy and Dave though. Not right now, not while everything with Holly was so fresh. I shrugged and let the conversation move along.

Chapter Fifteen

HOLLY

"What the hell do you mean?" Ella exclaimed. "Nate is the guy who spent five thousand dollars for a date with you?"

My cheeks burned, and I took a gulp of my wine. There was no real way to gloss over this.

"What? You didn't tell her?" Megan asked, her eyes wide.

I was at dinner in Anchorage with Ella and Megan. When Ella had called to invite me to go shopping with her for the weekend, I jumped at the opportunity. With thoughts about Nate practically burning holes in my brain, I needed something to keep my mind off of him.

Megan laughed and shook her head. "I don't know why you didn't bother to mention it. I mean, that makes it seem like a thing."

Meanwhile, Ella narrowed her green eyes, tucking her brown hair behind her ears. After a beat, she arched a brow, cocking her head to the side before sipping on her martini.

"Fine," I finally said. "I didn't want to get into it, but yeah. Nate claimed he was saving me from my other options."

Megan knocked back the rest of her martini and looked

between Ella and me. "That's what he said, but it's pretty obvious to me that he's got the hots for you."

Ella burst out laughing, slapping her palm on the table and drawing the attention of a few diners nearby. We were at Susitna Burgers & Brew, one of our favorite places to eat when we were here.

"Really? Is it necessary to get everyone's attention?" I asked with a sigh.

Ella shrugged before she started laughing again. After a moment, she got it under control. "No, but it's funny as hell. I told Caleb last year that Nate had a thing for you, and he agreed with me," she said, leaning forward. "In fact, Caleb said Nate *totally* had a thing for you back in high school."

The last bit of laughter faded from Ella's eyes. It was never easy to talk about high school. There was a blot on those memories because of the accident.

I was shocked, though. No one had ever mentioned Nate paying the least bit of attention to me back then. For what it's worth, I couldn't say I paid him too much attention, not in that way. He and Alex were best buds, just as they were now, and my twin brother had been all about annoying the hell out of me then. Nate mostly ignored Alex's teasing, but I lumped him in with Alex. Then, everything went to hell when Jake died, and we almost lost Ella too.

"Really?" I finally said.

"I don't know about back then," Megan cut in, "but that man seriously had a thing for you at the fundraiser. I'll give it to you, though, you were totally hot."

"Yeah, because you had me dressed up in the skimpiest nurse outfit *ever*."

"Are there any pictures?" Ella asked with a wink to Megan, who sat beside me.

"Oh yeah. Would you like one?" Megan countered.

"Jesus Christ, don't even," I muttered, although I was relieved not to dwell on high school. That subject was like a bruise. No matter how much time had passed, the dull ache was still there. "It was for a good cause, and I would do it all over again."

"Back to the important point, did you ever go on that date?" Ella asked.

"Yeah, he paid five grand," Megan said, her eyes wide. "It was a record."

I rolled my eyes, smirking at Ella. "The price drove up, I'm pretty sure he didn't start at that bid."

"Maybe so, but he was obviously willing to pay that much," she said with another roll of her eyes.

I knew Ella might be a little cranky that I kept this from her, but even worse, I felt like I was carrying a huge secret now. Although I hadn't told her about the potential date, that wasn't too much of a secret because it hadn't actually happened yet.

I'd never gotten around to fessing up to my way-too-late state of virginity. There had always seemed to be more important things going on. I mean, hell, after everything that went down in high school, things just fell by the wayside. Then, Ella moved away for years, and it was simply a conversation we never had.

Plus, it was kind of embarrassing. All that aside, now I'd gone a few steps ahead with Nate. I was holding a lot back now, though, Nate or not, and I didn't know what to do with it. I also wasn't so sure I wanted to talk about it. And yet, I needed advice. Badly.

Seeing as we were staying in a hotel just down the street and had walked here for dinner, I signaled the waitress, and we ordered another round of martinis. Conveniently, a friend Megan knew from town paused by the table to say hello. By the time all of that happened, our second round of drinks had arrived, and I took a few fortifying sips.

"Well, I guess I'll just spill it. I still haven't made good on my date, but I might've had a night with Nate," I said flatly.

Megan was mid-sip on her martini, and she sputtered

slightly before recovering. Ella's sharp green gaze swung to mine. "A night?"

"Sex," I offered bluntly in clarification.

Megan had just taken another sip of her drink and started coughing. I handed her a napkin while Ella stared at me, her eyes widening. "Oh God," she finally muttered.

"Why do you say it like that?" My tone came out sharper than I intended, but I was feeling defensive and insecure. My guess was Ella was worried Nate was going to treat me like he treated every other woman—someone to meet his needs for whatever time he allotted. I didn't mean to make Nate out to sound like a jerk. He wasn't. He kept things casual and hued to the likes of women who were happy to go along with it.

Getting involved with a friend within our small social circle was ripe for complications galore, and I damn well knew it.

Ella took a measured sip of her drink, her shoulders rising and falling with a breath. "Caleb thinks Nate's had a thing for you for years, but it doesn't change the fact that Nate's all about no strings. I don't want things to get messy. You're my best friend."

"It's not like I didn't walk into it with my eyes wide open," I finally said, promptly abandoning my plan to ask what I should do with all the feelings bubbling up inside of me. Because, oh sweet hell, there were feelings. I'd hardly been able to stop thinking about Nate since the other night and the morning after. His words when he departed rang in my mind.

"This isn't close to over."

Megan's gaze had sobered. "You know, it's not like I know Nate that well. Certainly not like you," she said, casting a glance at Ella before looking back to me. "He definitely had the hots for you, but casual isn't really the vibe I picked up. I thought he really liked you."

I lifted a shoulder in a tiny shrug, striving to keep my

tone nonchalant. "I don't know what Nate thinks. There's definitely chemistry. It's not like I can't handle myself. I don't have any expectations."

My mind was practically kicking and screaming at this point, and my heart was thumping loudly, almost in opposition of my words. I wanted more—so much more—with Nate, and I had to be damn careful to keep my expectations clear. "I don't know. I guess I'll just have to play it by ear. Don't worry," I added, glancing at Ella. "I'm a big girl. It's not like I don't know that Casual is Nate's middle name. It was one night. I'm not gonna read too much into it."

Ella opened her mouth as though to say something but then shut it, her lips pressing into a line. After a long moment, she appeared to reconsider her silence and said, "I thought you wanted something more with someone."

"Well, that'll come along when it does. Not everybody gets what you and Caleb have."

Something flickered in the depths of Ella's eyes. I knew she regretted how long she stayed away from Willow Brook, almost completely throwing away her chance of being with the love of her life. She finally nodded and took another sip of her martini. I knew she wanted to say more, but she obviously decided against it. I wasn't about to fess up to how much I had fantasized about Nate since our kiss last year. I had studiously avoided being alone with him out of fear of actually falling for him. I needed to remind myself that all I could ever expect from him was friends with benefits.

Megan caught my gaze, and I could see the worry contained in hers. I wasn't up for my friends worrying about me. With everything I'd been through, one thing I had fostered was being strong and independent. I wasn't about to fall apart over being stupid enough to so desperately want and need something from a man who was highly unlikely to give it to me. My excellent judgment in action.

Megan swiftly moved the topic on to other matters. After another round of drinks, Ella and I walked together back to the hotel, while Megan waved and hopped in a cab to go to her apartment. When we got back to our hotel room and changed into our pajamas, which consisted of sweatpants and comfy T-shirts, we lounged on the couch watching television.

Ella startled me when she spoke. "You really like him, don't you?"

She knew me too well for me to try to lie. My defenses were down, and I was tipsy from a few martinis. Rolling my head sideways on the back of the couch, I met her concerned gaze. "Maybe, but I'll be okay. Don't worry about me. Worrying is my job anyway. Don't try to take it away."

That had been my job for a long time in our friendship. We'd both been hit hard by what happened in the accident, but Ella had been the one driving. Although the accident was entirely the fault of the drunk driver who hit us, survivor's guilt had weighed heavily on her, more so than for Caleb and me, who had also been in the car.

She smiled softly, her laugh low in the quiet room. "Maybe so, but I get to worry too," she said, then her voice grew firm. "And I'll kick Nate's ass if he hurts you."

Chapter Sixteen

NATE

It was Sunday evening, and I was relieved I would be flying this group out the following morning. The weather looked good, so I hoped to be up in the air by sunrise. Being a little further north, the sun came up a little later. By my estimation and Dave's confirmation, I'd be wheels up before nine a.m.

I was dropping this group off in Anchorage, but then I would be flying my plane back to Willow Brook. This group has been dedicated to skiing all weekend, only appearing in the evenings inside the lodge. Dave, Nancy, and I were lounging in front of the fireplace, in one of the smaller collections of chairs in the main room. The television droned in the background while Dave and I finished a hand of rummy.

The main door into the lodge opened, voices filtering in as a group came inside. After they hung up their jackets and knocked the snow off their gear, they shuffled upstairs for showers. In short order, most of them were back downstairs where we all enjoyed a casual dinner of pizzas, courtesy of Nancy.

After we finished eating, we enjoyed more drinks in front of the fire. Aside from the single woman in the group I had transported here, there was another woman who'd flown in from Fairbanks, who was also quite the flirt. Yet again, I felt absolutely nothing. In fact, it grated on me slightly. Not that I had ever minded it, but there was definitely a theme of women traveling to Alaska to search out some rugged hunk of a man. It was a stereotype, one that Alaska had only fed into. There were a few reality shows, a calendar, and even a freaking magazine that leaned on that stereotype.

Seeing as I was usually looking for nothing more than passing flings, that label worked to my advantage. For the first time ever, I found the attention annoying. I wanted to shake it off. After I managed to lightly brush off the flirtations of one of the women, she spun away with a wink.

Dave's chuckle reached my ears, and I glanced in his direction. "What?" I asked.

Nancy leaned over to pick up her beer from the coffee table and shook her head. "You've never been short on women, but it seems to annoy you this time. Are you seeing someone?"

I honestly didn't know what the hell to say. I enjoyed visiting with Dave and Nancy. They were old friends and good people. They were also low drama, which was nice. This weekend had been different. I'd been hyperaware of the easy comfort they shared with each other, and the depth of commitment and love that was so evident between them.

They had been together more than a decade at this point, and nothing had faded. There was only one woman I had ever wanted to have that kind of comfort with—Holly. I had completely underestimated how quickly she would lasso my heart and cinch it tight.

When Nancy cleared her throat, I managed a casual shrug. "Not really, but dating does get old sometimes."

They both knew Holly, but I certainly wasn't up for going into that right now. Anything I had with her was so fresh that I didn't dare start talking about it. Not until I had a better sense of where things actually stood. One of the things I had always loved about Holly was how sassy and fiery she was. She had never been a woman to back down, and she was independent as all hell. Those very qualities I admired gave me pause. I walked a treacherous path between her viewing me as a man rather than a friend.

Dave chuckled. "Well, damn. Something tells me you just might want to settle down soon."

Oh, for fuck's sake. I loved having friends that I'd known since I was a kid, the kind of friends you knew you could count on, no matter what. That said, I didn't love having friends who could see right through me. With another shrug, I replied, "Maybe."

Nancy threw her head back with a laugh, nudging my knee with her foot. "Well, I've always said you'd make a damn good husband. Not for me, I just mean, I thought it was a waste."

"A waste?"

"You, wasting all your time on all these other women. That's all. You're a good man," she explained.

At that moment, two couples meandered over and conversation moved on. Blessedly, I might add.

That night, lying in bed, with a view out the window at the stars bright against the dark sky, Holly filled my thoughts and senses.

I'd had plenty of sex in my life. Yet, no experience had prepared me for that night with Holly. That night contained more than one first. Holly had held center stage in too many fantasies over the years. To have them come true rocked my world. It was also a first to experience intimacy that spun around us like a shimmering web, the filaments of silk cinching tighter and tighter. I'd been entirely unprepared for that.

The other first—the one that had kept me awake every night since—was that I couldn't get her out of my mind. The feel of her silken channel clenching around me, the sound of her husky voice, the rasp of her moans, the feel of her skin damp against mine and her lush curves pressed against me — all of it together, wrapped up into the hottest fucking night of my life.

I had wholly underestimated what it would feel like to actually *be* with her. I had also miscalculated the potential, oh-so-fucking messy complications if things didn't work out.

She had slayed me, completely ruined me for any other woman.

That night, alone in a bed in the middle of nowhere in Alaska, with nothing but the darkness, the stars, the mountains, and the icy winter air outside surrounding me, my cock ached simply replaying what it felt like to be with her in my mind.

I kicked the covers off, and strolled into the bathroom. A cold shower and my own hand brought me relief. Yet, it didn't satisfy my need. It barely scratched the surface.

———

The following afternoon, the sun was starting its bow in the sky as I lifted my small plane into the air in Anchorage and aimed west toward Willow Brook. I'd been in a rush to leave hours earlier, but one thing after another had slowed me down after we landed in Anchorage. The flight home was a hop, skip, and a jump. Within twenty minutes, with the ocean stretched out to one side and the mountains on the other, a valley opened up, and I could see Swan Lake shimmering under the gold and orange of the setting sun.

In short order, I had landed at the small runway on the outskirts of town and was putting my plane away in the hangar. The sound of the door opening echoed through the cavernous space. "Nate," Caleb's voice called.

Slinging my backpack over my shoulder, I rounded the plane. "Hey man, what's up?" I asked as he approached.

Caleb and I shared the same coloring. His brown hair was rumpled, likely from a busy day fighting some kind of fire somewhere, or perhaps rescuing someone. My older brother was definitely a stereotype—a hotshot-firefighter-save-the-day kind of guy. I loved to tease him about it, but I wouldn't trade him as a brother for the world.

Caleb stopped by the plane as I let my backpack slide to the floor, and I rested my hips against the cockpit door. "Not much. Saw your truck and thought I'd see if you wanted to swing by Wildlands to catch a drink with the guys."

Normally, this would be an easy yes. I was on edge and could use the time to wind down with friends. I'd been too damn restless to get here and see Holly. I wanted to drive straight to her place, yet I was fucking starving. In this case, though, one need ran roughshod over the other. I needed to see Holly. Sooner rather than later. My need for her was more pressing than air, water, or food. Catching Caleb's eyes, I shook my head. "I gotta run home and grab a shower. I'm pretty beat."

I was lying through my teeth. I'd had a shower this morning. Although I wasn't lying about the fact that I was tired, I sure as hell wasn't too tired to go track Holly down with every intention of getting skin-to-skin with her as soon as feasibly possible.

If Caleb picked up on anything, he let it slide and simply shrugged. "Suit yourself."

I pushed my hips away from the plane, leaning over to snag my backpack again. We started walking out together in silence. I sensed something was on Caleb's mind, but I didn't know what. After I locked up the hangar, we walked toward our trucks together. He paused at the passenger side of mine as I opened the door and tossed my backpack on the seat.

"I figure I better let you know that Ella will kick your fucking ass—her words, not mine—if you hurt Holly," Caleb said flatly.

Oh fuck. This could only mean one thing. Holly must've said something to Ella about us.

Turning, I closed the door and rested my hand on the hood as I glanced to Caleb. "She'll kick my fucking ass?" I countered.

Caleb bit back a laugh and nodded. He didn't add anything else, and I figured he was waiting to see what I would say.

"Look, I don't know what Ella knows..." I let my words trail off when Caleb flashed a wide grin.

"Well, she knows you had sex with Holly because I got an earful about it. Let me tell you, the last thing I want is a lecture about my brother's sex life."

"Oh, for fuck's sake," I muttered, running a hand through my hair.

"Dude, I don't care to know the details. But you know how Ella is. She's all protective and doesn't want to see Holly get hurt. Plus, she thinks Holly wants something serious and isn't so sure it's a good idea for you two to be hooking up. Again, none of my business, but I do get her point. You're not exactly interested in anything more. Never have been."

Staring at Caleb, I sighed. "I know. It's not like that with Holly. She means something. I'm just not so sure she'll believe me."

I could *not* fucking believe I was having this conversation. It wasn't as if my brother and I didn't have serious conversations. We'd always been close. Also, with everything that Caleb went through after the accident in high school, it got us over any lingering anxieties about tackling heavy topics. That had been some seriously heavy shit, and we'd made it through to the other side.

Truth was, back when I'd been in high school, I hadn't said a word to anybody about my crush on Holly. The very accident that put us through the fire as far as talking about heavy subjects made it so many other things didn't get addressed.

Seeing as I had all but dedicated myself to casual relationships after that, I certainly hadn't had conversations about romance with Caleb. When I met his gaze, I saw a mixture of understanding and a hint of amusement.

"Go ahead and laugh," I said, circling my hand in the air and turning to rest my hips against my truck.

Caleb chuckled. "Does Holly know?"

"Know what?"

"That you want something more than casual?"

Leaning my head back to look at the sky, I took a deep breath, letting it out before I leveled my gaze with Caleb's. "I don't think so."

Caleb shook his head. "Well, you've got your work cut out for you. Not to mention, I wonder what Alex is going to think of all this."

I groaned. "So am I."

"True, but she's your best friend's twin sister. Your reputation precedes you. You might want to head him off at the pass before he gets the wrong idea."

"Right. That makes perfect sense. But I can't exactly do that without making sure Holly's okay with it. She'll fucking read me the riot act if I start talking without her say-so. Although, I guess it's okay for her to gossip to her friends," I muttered.

Caleb chuckled. "Saying something to her best friend isn't quite gossip. I'd let that one slide. You know Ella won't say a thing to anyone. She only said something to me because we're married. Well, and I guess she thought I'd keep you in line. I'll have to tell her there's nothing to worry about."

Eyeing Caleb, I shrugged. "Definitely not."

He was quiet, his gaze assessing. After a few beats, he chuckled again. "I'll see you around then. Mom and Dad want to have dinner this weekend, you coming?" he asked as he turned toward his truck.

"Of course. I'll see you then, if not sooner."

Chapter Seventeen

NATE

I turned onto Main Street in downtown Willow Brook. I didn't know if this was flat-out crazy, but I was going to see Holly. Now.

When I pulled up behind her building and cut my engine, I sat in silence for a moment. Need was already thrumming through me—a restlessness to see her, to lose myself in her, driving me.

I had no idea what to expect from her, or if she cared to see me. Climbing out of my truck, the cold winter air was almost a relief. The sharpness hit my senses and opened them wide.

I knocked on her kitchen door and waited. I assumed she was home because her car was here, but she also could've walked to Wildlands or Firehouse Café. I happened to know her preferred hangouts, if only because I'd known her forever.

Just enough time passed between when I knocked and I heard her footsteps approaching the door that I started to wonder if she wasn't here. A sense of disappointment slammed into me.

When I heard her approach, a breath I hadn't known I'd been holding slipped out in a sigh. There was a peephole on her door, and I saw her eye looking through. I knew she wasn't a fan of drop-ins, and I wondered if she would simply ignore me. It was clear she wasn't expecting me when she opened the door. She wore a long T-shirt that hung halfway down her thighs and a pair of bulky, blue fuzzy socks.

With her cheeks flushed and her brown eyes wide, it took all of my restraint not to kiss her right then and there.

"Hey," I said after a weighted moment of silence.

Holly stared at me, her tongue darting out and swiping across her bottom lip, sending a jolt of blood straight to my already swollen cock. I didn't even want to contemplate what it meant that nothing more than the thought of seeing Holly had me hard on the drive over here. She made me feel like a young kid who had no control. I supposed when it came to her, I didn't. My eyes flicked down— because they were greedy and needed to absorb the sight of her. Her nipples were taut, visible through her thin cotton T-shirt.

The rest of her lush body was hidden, but my mind filled in the blanks. I knew the soft give of her flesh when my hands were gripping her hips and now knew she had freckles scattered here and there, all over her.

That was something I'd gotten to learn about her a few nights ago. She had a dusting of freckles across her nose and cheeks, but I hadn't known she had random freckles sprinkled over her body, a map of constellations for me to explore. Because I needed, fucking needed, to know every inch of her.

"Hi," she belatedly said. "What are you doing here?"

Fair question. I didn't even think, my answer just came out. "I just got back. I wanted to see you." A gust of cold wind cut across the landing outside her kitchen, blowing through her door. Her shiver was visible. "Can I come in?"

"Oh, of course." She stepped back, opening the door

wider to let me through. Her scent drifted up to me—sweet and sharp, just like her.

Closing the door behind us, she turned, staying right where she was beside the door. Crossing her arms, she asked, "How was your trip?"

"Fine."

Words, emotions, and need jostled for space inside my brain. Need won out. I couldn't even manage polite conversation.

The air felt electric around us. Maybe a foot separated us, and the need to touch her beat inside me like a drum. I didn't want to talk. My common sense tried to speak up, but it was washed away in the current of raw lust. I reached out, catching one of her hands in mine.

If she had hesitated, even a little, I'm sure I would've been sensible. But she didn't. Her hand curled into mine as her arms fell away, and I stepped closer. I could see the wild flutter of her pulse in her neck.

Stepping closer, I released her hand to brush her hair away from her face, my fingers sliding through her silky hair and down her spine to cup the lush curve of her ass. She came flush against me, her breath hissing through her teeth on a gasp.

"What are you doing, Nate?"

"I missed you," I murmured, my lips dusting across her cheek. I nipped at her ear, savoring the subtle ripple that ran through her and the feel of her skin pebbling under my lips.

She gasped when my teeth grazed the soft skin on her neck. I could practically feel the thoughts bouncing around in her brain. Then, I felt when she stopped thinking. I dragged my tongue along her neck, relishing the feel of her nipples tight against my chest through the thin fabric of her T-shirt and mine. When I made my way up to claim her lips, she sighed, her entire body relaxing.

Our kiss was a sizzling point of contact, like lightning striking dry grass. The fire was instantaneous. Our kiss went wild—her tongue tangling with mine as a low rumble ran through her. I held her fast against me, palming her ass and rocking my arousal into the cradle of her hips.

Holly had all but built a fucking house in my thoughts. I hadn't thought through what it would feel like to be with her again. I was too caught up in nothing but instinct and sensation for this to be anything other than that—pure, raw, and elemental. Holly called to every fiber of me. The sense of relief that rolled through me at feeling the depth of her response was intense and only fed the fire threatening to engulf us.

She shoved at my jacket, and I shrugged it loose, reaching behind my head to yank my shirt off. I stepped back only long enough to catch the hem of her T-shirt and lift it up and over her head, tossing it to the floor where it joined mine.

My eyes flicked down to find that she was bare naked, not even a pair of panties. Well, except her socks, which were downright endearing.

"Jesus, Holly, you're walking around without underwear?"

She gasped when I reached out, cupping my hand between her thighs and feeling a tease of her wet heat there. Her skin was flushed all over. Dipping my head, I caught one of her nipples with my mouth, swirling my tongue and sucking it hard and fast, savoring the sharp sting of her hands in my hair, gripping tightly as she cried out.

She was drenched, her slick desire coating my fingers as I teased through her folds. Lifting my head, I caught her eyes. "You're fucking soaked."

When I sank two fingers inside of her, knuckle deep, she moaned. "Oh God, Nate."

"Tell me something," I murmured.

"What?"

I stepped closer, and her head thumped against the door as I drew my fingers out and sank them inside of her again. "Did you miss me?"

Her gaze held mine, her eyes widening with a hint of that feisty stubbornness that I loved so fucking much. When she didn't answer, I drew my fingers out again, teasing at the slick heat of her entrance. Then, I drove them deep and she cried out.

"Yes!" she almost shouted.

I was crazed. I hadn't meant for this to be anything but hot and fast, but I needed her—all of her. Now. With one hand steadying her hip, I sank to my knees in front of her. Hooking one of her legs over my shoulders, I buried my face between her thighs. She was salty and sweet and so wet, I almost came in my jeans. My cock was straining against my zipper, but I needed this first. I needed to feel her come against my mouth.

Fucking her slowly with my fingers and exploring every inch of her with my tongue, she was at the edge in a matter of seconds.

"Oh my God! Oh my God, don't stop," she ordered me.

When I grazed my teeth over her clit, my name came out in a broken shout as her hips bucked against my mouth, her entire body tightening and shuddering. I didn't wait, drawing back swiftly and freeing my cock as I lifted her against me, using the wall behind us to support her.

Gripping my cock in my fist, I dragged it through her wet folds, pausing to catch my breath. It was then, as I slid the underside of my cock against her swollen clit, that remembered I hadn't even bothered to make sure if I had any condoms with me.

"Fuck," I muttered, starting to draw back.

Holly's legs tightened around me, holding me in place. "Where are you going?"

I fumbled in my back pocket with my jeans hanging half off, figuring I had to have something in my wallet. Awareness dawned in her eyes, and her lips curled in a smile. "I'm a nurse. I'm on the shot and clean as can be."

My gaze slammed into hers. I'd never had sex without a

condom. I'd been subjected to my father's blunt sex talk before I even finished middle school.

"I've never had sex without a condom," I finally said.

Holly's grin expanded and she leaned her head back against the door. With her hair a messy tousle around her face, her brown eyes dark with desire, and her lips swollen and puffy from our kisses, she was so damn sexy, it took all I had not to bury myself.

"Of course you haven't," she said with a husky laugh. "You're a good boy like that." Her gaze sobered. "Fuck me."

I immediately discovered that, when it came to Holly, I was quite good at following orders. With my jeans hanging around my hips and her bare save for her bright blue socks, I adjusted my angle and sank home inside of her.

Her slick, clenching heat felt so damn good, I had to hold still and count to ten to keep from blowing my load right then and there.

Chapter Eighteen

HOLLY

Nate's gruff voice drew my eyes open. My gaze collided with his. With my back against the door, the cool wood was a contrast to his heat pressed against me. The feel of him filling me was so damn good, I could barely think beyond anything but the pleasure spiraling inside.

He held still for a few beats and then rocked his hips, just barely, into the cradle of mine, sending a jolt of hot pleasure from my core radiating through me. I hadn't expected to see him tonight. Much as I wouldn't have wanted to admit it to anyone, I'd been counting the days, the hours, the minutes, and the seconds until I knew he would be back. Which was completely and utterly ridiculous.

I'd never viewed myself as the kind of woman who would ever get hung up on anxiously waiting for a man to return. He'd been gone a mere few days. I had hoped my trip to Anchorage would keep me occupied. Total fail. I had been occupied in the practical sense of the word. Yet, Nate had never been far from my thoughts. Not even a little. He had always been there, waiting in the wings to stroll through. My mind and body replayed my night with him probably a few hundred times in the three days that had passed in the interim.

It felt as if he were imprinted onto my body and burned into my senses. To have him here now, taking me against the door, it was everything I wanted and more.

With his eyes locked to mine, he adjusted me in his arms. He held me easily, not exactly a surprise. Ever since my body's antenna had tuned into Nate, I was far too aware of how ridiculously fit he was—all hard muscle, rugged, and roguish. Just now, he had one hand gripping my hip and the other cupped underneath my bottom. With his bare chest brushing against my breasts, it occurred to me I could orgasm from that sensation alone. He drew back more fully and sank in again, lifting me a little higher against the door.

"So," he murmured, his gaze burning into mine, peeling away what little barriers I had, flimsy though they were, "here's the thing. I couldn't stop thinking about you this weekend. The other night was not all we're having. This"— he paused, his hips shifting back and surging forward, the glide of his cock inside me eliciting a moan—"is happening now, later, and probably tomorrow morning. Tell me you don't want this."

On the heels of a ragged breath, he drew his hips back once again, filling and stretching me so exquisitely I could hardly bear it. All this time I'd been craving Nate, I hadn't imagined it could be like this. With each stroke into my slick core, his pelvis barely brushed against my clit, striking like flint to stone on the bundle of nerves.

Even though I'd been a virgin until a few days ago, it wasn't as if I had been entirely inexperienced, it's just that I'd never made it to the act of completion. Even then, I knew without question that I had never felt anything even remotely close to what I felt with Nate.

His expert fingers and mouth had sent me flying once already tonight, and now his words and his cock were sending me over the edge again as the pressure built from the embers of my last climax. My legs were curled around him as if my life depended on it as I chased after another release.

"You didn't answer," he murmured, his eyes narrowing.

Through the fog of lust clouding my brain, I stared at him.

"Tell me you want this as much as I do." The gruff sound of his voice alone sent a hot shiver straight up my spine, a sweet ache building at my core.

"Of course I do," I finally murmured with a low cry on the heels of a deep stroke.

"Look at me," Nate murmured, the sound of his voice flickering along my overwrought nerves.

Dragging my eyes open, I met his gaze, dark and intent. I didn't know how to read what I saw in his eyes.

I didn't remember not knowing Nate. And yet, what had passed between us in the last few days was such a shift in our connection to each other, it felt as if we were on a new plane entirely. He adjusted me in his arms, lifting me higher against the door as he drove into me again. With his gaze searing into mine, my heart thudded hard and fast in my chest. His strength and heat surrounded me. I felt as if we were alone in the world, caught in a shimmering web of intimacy, need, and pure pleasure.

My eyes started to fall closed as he drew back, the slow glide sending sparks of pleasure scattering through me. "Look at me," he murmured again, the warm command in his tone clear.

A spark flared inside. I wanted to argue. Opening my eyes, I met his gaze as he held still, the thick head of his cock teasing me at my entrance. "What if I said no?"

A corner of his mouth curled up, the heat in his gaze nearly burning me. "I wouldn't give you what you wanted until you did," he countered.

I started to reply, but then he filled me and whatever I meant to say came out in a low moan.

"I want you to know exactly who's inside you when you fly apart again. I want to feel you coming all over my cock."

His words, so blunt and dirty, sent a thrill through me. I couldn't have looked away if I wanted to now. It was almost a dare, as if I were going to shy away from it. He didn't rush. With the cool wood of the door against my back, he fucked me slowly and intently, his pelvis rocking against my clit with every thrust.

Each time, shards of pleasure shot through me. Toeing the edge of another climax, I shuddered, chasing after my release with Nate's eyes locked to mine. On another surge, when he filled me deeply, my over-sensitized nerves snapped, fire flashing through me as I trembled in ecstasy.

He drew back, surging into me again, his hips pounding hard and fast. I barely registered the force of it, the line between pleasure and pain blurring. His name fell in a breathy chant from my lips as I felt the heat of his release filling me, my own name a rough shout from him on the heels of a guttural cry.

I was spinning, pleasure rushing through me, around me, and inside me as I tried to catch my breath. The only anchor holding me to reality was the feel of Nate clutching me fast against him.

Still holding me, his head fell into the dip of my neck, his breath gusting across my skin. My own breath came in ragged gasps as I tried to pull myself together. I didn't want to move. I wanted to stay held in his strong embrace, lost in this web of need and intimacy that I had never imagined, much less with Nate.

After a few moments, I felt him shift as he lifted his head. At that moment, his stomach growled. He chuckled, a rueful smile teasing his lips as I dragged my eyes open. Reality snapped me into motion. I started to move, but he held me close. Leaning my head back, I cocked it to the side. "Are you gonna let me down?"

My cheeks felt hot. The heat of the moment, so to

speak, had passed and reality was coming at me hard and fast.

"I am, but first..." Leaning forward, he caught my lips in a swift kiss. His tongue slid in to tangle against mine for a moment before he drew away again. Just like that, my body tingled all over again.

He didn't say anything else, he simply drew out of me slowly and eased me down. I was shaking, and my body was still reverberating from a succession of two intense orgasms. I felt wrung dry with pleasure. Emotion was hot on its heels, emotion I didn't quite want to face.

I thanked the stars I had the door behind me to hold me up. Placing my palms flat against it, I suddenly felt bare inside. I *was* bare all over with the exception of my socks.

Nate didn't step far away and stood there, his eyes on me. Oh geez. He was just ridiculous with his jeans hanging open and his rather generous cock visible. My eyes greedily tracked over him. If my body had its way, we'd go for another round.

Conveniently, his stomach rumbled again, giving my common sense a moment to assert itself. With my legs still shaky, I pushed away from the door. "Are you hungry?"

"Clearly," he said, with just enough sarcasm in his tone that it prodded my snarky side to life.

"Were you silly enough not to bother to get something to eat before you came over?" I asked as I strolled past him, fetching my T-shirt off the floor and slipping it over my head quickly.

When I turned back, he was buttoning his jeans and shrugging into his shirt.

"I didn't care about food. I wanted to see you more than I wanted to eat."

My common sense didn't last very long. My heart practically sat up and clapped at that comment. Next thing I knew, I was suggesting we order pizza. Even though it was close to dark, I hadn't eaten yet either.

"Sounds good," he replied.

"I'll order," I said quickly as he started to slide his phone out of his pocket.

Willow Brook was a very small town. Well, maybe not that small. But I didn't doubt for a second that if Nate put in the order, word would somehow travel that he was here at my apartment. He paused, his finger hovering over his phone screen.

"I can get it." As he looked at me, his gaze cleared. "You're worried someone might notice I'm here."

My cheeks heated, and I didn't care. "Yeah, yeah, I am. Alex is your best friend, and I'm not quite ready for him to know what's going on with us."

Nate's hand dropped, and he slipped his phone back into his pocket. "Understood," he said with a nod, and I raised my eyebrows.

His laugh sent a shiver skating over my skin as I turned, walking to the kitchen to get my phone off the counter. Hitching my hip on a stool, I looked back at him. "What's so funny?"

"You were ready for a fight, weren't you?"

I rolled my eyes and stuck my tongue out at him, something I'd probably done a few hundred times in our lives. "So what if I was? Moving on, what kind of pizza do you want? I'm ordering from Alpenglow Pizza. It's my new favorite."

"I'll eat whatever."

I should've known that would be his answer. Because Nate would eat whatever I wanted. He wasn't a picky eater. At all.

"Okay, then half pepperoni and half Greek because I want both."

While I was on the phone, he finally kicked off his shoes and fetched his jacket from the floor to hang it on the hook by the door. As I waited for the woman taking our order to finish another call, he stepped behind me, slipping his hands around my waist and dipping his head to dust kisses along the side of my neck.

Butterflies spun in my belly and my channel clenched. Oh dear God. I was already in over my head, so deep I was practically drowning.

Chapter Nineteen

HOLLY

A few days passed, during which I kept reminding myself of the plain truth and the contradiction within it. I couldn't fall for Nate. Yet, I was falling—hard and fast—for Nate.

I suppose the truth was I had already been deep in danger of falling for him ever since our first tipsy, fuzzy, madness-infused kiss from over a year ago now, in a coat closet at a party. Then, I had to go to that stupid fundraiser. I had regained my footing before that night. Thinking back, I figured I could've recovered if nothing else happened.

Then, there was *the elevator incident*, as I'd come to call it in my mind. By that point, I was lost. And now? Well, now, far too much had happened.

The second day of February dawned cold and clear. Groundhog Day. I woke in the darkness, wide-awake, and hot and bothered over a dream about Nate. After our second night together, I'd had two night shifts in a row. It had been convenient for my sanity, if only because it saved me from having to purposefully avoid seeing him.

I'd never thought much about his work schedule. When

I came awake with my skin flushed and my panties wet, I instantly wished he was with me. Sweet hell.

I wonder if he's working today. Oh my God. You need to stop wondering about Nate and his fucking work schedule.

I'd never wondered about any man's work schedule. Which made this all the more embarrassing.

Nate ran his own business and took flights as he pleased. I knew summers were busier for him because they were busier for any backcountry pilot in Alaska. Come winter, he did contract work for a few local airlines out of Anchorage and flew adventurers out into the backcountry for ski trips and the like.

Restless, I kicked the covers off and hurried to the shower. Much as my body was begging for it, I refused to give in and find release at my own hand with nothing but Nate filling my thoughts.

Although, I had done that a few hundred times in the last year or so. So fucking embarrassing. With the hot water practically scalding me, I washed away my dream, but I had no luck kicking Nate out of my mind. He filled every corner of it.

Normally, when I had an early shift like I did today, I would have coffee at home and maybe grab a bowl of cereal before I went in to the hospital. Today, however, being alone with my thoughts made me restless. Once I was dressed, I stuffed my feet into my winter boots, shrugged on my down jacket, and headed out to grab coffee and a breakfast sandwich at Firehouse Café. Those who lived through long winters often came to the conclusion that one of the best inventions ever known to humankind was the remote start for cars. I had tapped mine on while I was still getting dressed and climbed into a nice, toasty car a few minutes later.

Within minutes, I pulled up in front of Firehouse Café just down the street. In the summer, I would've walked, but I was no glutton for punishment. It was still dark out, with the stars still bright in the sky and a pretty, curved slice of the moon sitting above the mountains behind downtown Willow Brook.

I took a deep breath of the bracing air as my footsteps crunched across the snowy parking lot. The lights twinkled in the windows, beckoning me inside. Pushing through the door, warmth and the scent of coffee and baked goods spun around me, infusing my senses.

Despite the early hour, there were a few people here, and I could hear the bustle in the kitchen behind the swinging doors into the back. Walking to the counter, I grinned at Janet when she looked up.

"Morning, Holly," she said with a wide smile. She set aside the scones she had been bagging up. "What can I get for you this morning?"

"I'll take an Americano and an egg sandwich."

"Coming right up." Turning, she called over the door into the back. "Hey Daniel, mind coming out here to get an egg sandwich ready?"

The café was set up so that there was a grill visible behind the counter, while the baking happened in the back. Daniel pushed through the doors, throwing a grin my way and quickly turning to the grill.

Janet got started on my coffee, casting another smile my way before looking to the door when the bell chimed. "Hey there, Jake and Sandy," she called.

Turning, I saw Jake Green's parents approaching me. All through the horrible aftermath of Jake's death in high school, they had remained fixtures in Willow Brook. Like me, they'd walked through the fire of that grief and made it out to the other side.

"Morning, Holly," Sandy said as she tugged me close for a quick hug.

Jake winked and nodded as he caught his wife's hand back in his. "You must have a morning shift at the hospital," he observed.

"You got it," I replied.

I had stayed friendly with Jake's parents all these years. I'd known them since I was a little girl. Out of everyone in Willow Brook, they had the clearest understanding of what my relationship with Jake had been. I thanked my stars for that because I couldn't imagine having to try to explain that to them.

Sandy brushed her dark hair back from her face, casting a smile at Janet when she turned to hand me my coffee.

"Let me guess, two coffees for you?" Janet asked.

"Of course," Jake replied.

"Anything to eat?"

"No thanks. We're headed to Anchorage for some errands today, and I've got a doctor's appointment."

"Everything okay?" Janet asked over her shoulder as she prepped their coffees.

"Oh yes, just a mammogram. You know how fun those are."

Janet barked a laugh. At that moment, I heard my brother's voice through the door as it opened, a gust of cold air blowing in with him. Lo and behold, Nate was right behind him.

Oh fuck. Alex knew nothing of what happened between Nate and me. Conveniently, our paths hadn't crossed too much in the last week or so.

Alex must've heard the tail end of our conversation. His eyes flicked between me, Janet, and Sandy. Sandy shrugged and threw a wry grin his way. "Yes, you did just hear me say mammogram. It's okay, nothing you ever have to look forward to," she said with a little laugh. Meanwhile, Jake rolled his eyes, shaking his head.

"Um, okay then," Alex replied.

It was rare to see my twin brother at a loss for words, especially when it came to inappropriate jokes. But this one was definitely out of his territory. I grinned. "Morning."

The moment had been just enough to nudge me out of

my self-consciousness with encountering Alex and Nate together this morning.

Nate's eyes caught mine, the glint held within sending a curl of heat through my veins.

Oh geez. This was so fucking unfair. My body needed an off switch when it came to Nate. I was standing here with the parents of my old high school boyfriend and my twin brother who was Nate's best friend. The entire situation should've thrown ice water on any desire I had for Nate.

It didn't. Not at all.

Fuck my life.

I managed a tight smile in Nate's direction and hoped like hell the heat I felt in my cheeks was subtle enough that no one else noticed it. Janet turned back, and I fished my wallet out of my purse as she passed the coffees to Sandy and Jake.

"I need to pay you," I said, handing over a five.

"Gotcha." Janet took it from me quickly and rang me up.

"Just put the change in the tip jar," I added.

With a smile, she tossed it in, her attention turning to Nate and Alex while she rang up Jake and Sandy. Meanwhile, Daniel handed me my egg sandwich on a plate. Only minutes ago, sitting down to enjoy my coffee and breakfast in silence would have been nice. Now, I wanted to flee. They were too many confusing thoughts bouncing around in my brain, competing for space with my emotions, which were threatening to overrun everything.

Unfortunately, there was no graceful way to make it happen, especially not when Alex spoke. "Perfect, you're going to have breakfast with me, right?" he asked.

"I guess so," I replied, thinking there was no other good answer.

Plate and coffee in hand, I paused beside Sandy and Jake. "Good to see you two this morning. How is Clay?" I asked, referring to Jake's younger brother.

"Oh, he's great. He's in Washington D.C. doing an

internship," Sandy replied, her pride evident. "We're going to go visit him in a couple of weeks. We haven't been to D.C. since we went as chaperones on his high school trip there." Sandy dropped a kiss on my cheek. "Always good to see you, dear."

I waved as they exited, turning to glance back at Alex and Nate. Alex was teasing him about something as Nate paid for their coffees. "I'll grab a table, guys," I said quickly, before turning and striding toward a table in the far corner by the windows.

Normally, it wouldn't be a thing for me to run into my brother and his best friend here. Although Alex wasn't much of a morning person, his job as a specialized mechanic often meant he was up and about early. Like me, Nate had always been an early riser. Running into him here in the morning was a fairly common occurrence and shouldn't have affected me. Yet, being anywhere near Nate's vicinity set me on fire inside.

I couldn't help but wonder if he had a trip scheduled. Just seeing him had my body humming. I didn't need to contemplate how awkward and inconvenient it was to have the hots for my brother's best friend. It wasn't as if this was a new state of being. The difference was I had acted on it, or rather, *we* had acted on it. Now, it felt quite real and much more intense than I had imagined.

I settled into a chair and took a long sip of my coffee. Slivers of light were rising above the mountains in the distance. It would be another hour or so before light claimed the darkness completely. Just in time for me to start my shift at work.

After another sip of coffee, I took a bite of my sandwich, glancing up when Nate slipped into the chair across from me. Alex was nowhere in sight. "Where's Alex?"

"Bathroom." He paused, his gaze dark and inscrutable as he regarded me. I wanted to kiss him, but quickly shoved that thought away. "Morning shift?"

"Yup." The implications of my answer suddenly hit me. I had legitimately worked the last two night shifts. My work schedule had been my easy out for not seeing Nate. Since he now knew I had a day shift today, I had no convenient way to avoid seeing him tonight if he asked.

Heat flooded my belly, radiating through me. Nate took a sip of his coffee, his gaze never breaking from mine. The promise contained there set my pulse to pounding and took my breath away. My mind spun to...

At that moment, Alex arrived, effectively bringing a screeching halt to my train of thought.

Get a grip.

My internal order sounded bossy and clear, but my body was in outright revolt and ignored it entirely.

Alex hooked his hand on a chair at the table beside us, swinging it over and sitting down. "Early shift, sis?"

"Of course. Why else would I be here at this hour in my scrubs?"

Alex took a swig of his coffee and chuckled. "Point taken."

"What's your schedule today? You're never up at this hour voluntarily."

"So true. I'm handling a major repair on an engine at the airport in Anchorage, so I need an early start. I sweet-talked Nate into going with me, and maybe a double date," Alex said, cutting his gaze to Nate.

Conversation along these lines between my brother and Nate had happened many a time in my presence. Until the last year or so, I'd never thought much of it. Now, hot jealousy shot through me, and anxiety churned in my gut.

Note to self: this is why you never should've let anything happen with Nate.

I couldn't help it, but my eyes slid to Nate. I forced myself to look away just as quickly, glancing out the window, praying that none of my feelings showed on my face.

"Dude, I already told you I'm not spending the night. I'm definitely not up for a date. You're flying solo," Nate said.

Oh my God. This was awful. I wanted to ask what any of this meant. We hadn't spoken about what had happened between us. Not that I blamed Nate for that. I sure as hell didn't want to talk about it, not when I couldn't form a coherent thought when it came to him and my feelings. Layering into the awkwardness was the extremely inconvenient audience of my brother.

I took a big bite of my egg sandwich, pouring my muddled emotions into chewing furiously.

Alex shrugged easily. "Fine, man, your loss. What's the deal with you, though? Haven't you noticed he's off his game? It's like he's sworn off women," Alex said, directing his observation to me.

Taking a gulp of my coffee, I shrugged because that was about all I had to offer on this topic. Alex rolled his eyes and I took another bite of my sandwich, willing myself not to look at Nate. I resolved not to let anything else happen between us because these kinds of conversations were going to continue to suck. Regardless of why he was saying no to Alex's offer of a double date—whatever the hell that meant —I was under no illusions that he took anything between us seriously.

Somehow, I managed to get through the rest of that rather awkward and miserable few minutes. Seeing as neither Alex nor Nate knew precisely when I was supposed to show up at the hospital, as soon as I finished my sandwich, I stood. "Gotta go, guys. Have a good trip to Anchorage. Catch you later."

I didn't wait, slinging my purse over my shoulder and hurrying out. Just as I was about to reach my car, I heard footsteps behind me, a subtle crunch on the packed snow in the parking lot.

"Holly."

The sound of Nate's voice in the cold, quiet winter

morning sent a jolt through me. I was spinning inside, caught in a riptide of emotion, self-judgment, and confusion, all of it mingling with that initial surge of desire. I *so* wanted to ignore him, but I knew I couldn't quite get away with it. Taking a steadying breath, I stopped beside my car and glanced back. "Yeah?"

He had closed the distance between us. One more stride, and he was immediately in front of me. The force of his presence was potent. It was cold, and he emanated warmth. I didn't say anything, mostly because I didn't quite trust myself.

"None of that was my idea," he said, his gaze intent.

I felt as if he was trying to see right through me. Not that it would've mattered if he could. I couldn't make any sense of my own feelings. There was a jostle of emotion and reason bouncing all over the place inside.

I shrugged. When he didn't say anything else, I felt compelled to fill the silence. "It's no big deal. It's not like you owe me an explanation," I finally said.

Something flickered in his gaze. Through the wispy gray of the winter dawn, I couldn't see into his eyes very well. I also didn't trust my own perception, not when it was colored by a mess of emotions.

"I do owe you an explanation. I'm not seeing anyone. I haven't for—" He paused, leaning his head back to look up into the sky. When he leveled his gaze with mine again, the air misted with his sigh. "I haven't seen anybody since before last Halloween."

His words hit me right in the solar plexus. That was months ago now. Halloween had been the night of the fundraiser. My mouth opened and closed. I felt like a damn fish.

His lips curled at one corner, and he shrugged. "You're my priority."

"Huh?"

Brilliant, Holly.

I elected to ignore my ever-ready critical voice.

His shoulders rose and fell with a deep breath. "Okay, I'm going to give it to you straight. I can imagine you have your reasons for thinking otherwise, but this is far more than just sex for me. I want you. In every way."

His words were low, his gaze resolved. My heart banged inside my chest, trying to break free from the cage of my ribs. I shook my head, because I didn't quite believe it, nor did I know how to react to any of this.

The door to Firehouse Café opened across the parking lot. Alex was stepping out, his back to us as he spoke to someone inside.

Nate stepped to me, bending low and pressing his lips to mine. The kiss was brief and electrifying. The contrast of the icy morning air and the feel of his lips against mine was so sharp, pleasure pierced through me. Panic followed swiftly because when I looked up, Alex had turned. I didn't know what he had seen.

Nate shrugged, his eyes searching mine as he straightened. "I don't care what Alex thinks. You shouldn't either. This is between you and me."

For a woman who wasn't usually at a loss for words, this moment did it. All I could do was stare at him.

"Go to work," he said softly, reaching past me to open the door to my car.

Despite my mental haze, I had tapped the remote start button in the café before I walked out. A blast of heat hit me as the car door opened.

"I'll be by tonight," Nate said, his voice low enough for no one but me to hear it.

Somehow, I climbed in my little car, and Nate closed the door behind me. I watched as he turned to walk toward Alex, where their trucks were parked, side by side. Alex waved and then they drove away, with Nate following Alex.

What the hell just happened here?

Chapter Twenty

NATE

"What the hell is going on with you and my sister?" Alex demanded, slamming the door shut behind him as we entered the large plane hangar.

I was damn surprised Alex had made it this long without asking me anything about Holly. When she practically ran out of Firehouse Café this morning, I had said to hell with it in my mind and followed her. I wasn't going to let her go through the day assuming that I was even remotely interested in dating anyone else.

I knew I was taking a chance, one that might piss Holly off more than anyone. I didn't give a damn if Alex was pissed off at me. I would deal with it.

He stopped walking, turning to face me. No one else was around. Two small planes sitting in the hangar were our only audience. Metal walls and concrete made for an echoing space.

I met his gaze head-on. "What do you mean?"

I didn't mind the confrontation. In fact, I knew it had to come at some point. Might as well get it over with. I wouldn't have minded more time to figure out just how much to say to my best friend about the fact I was on the way to being in love with his twin sister.

Alex cocked his head to the side, narrowing his eyes. "You know exactly what I mean. I saw you kiss her this morning. She was tense as hell at breakfast. She's not gonna tell me, so you better."

"I'm not sure yet," I finally said. "But I'd like to see where things go."

"Fuck," Alex muttered. "You can't fuck my sister over. You don't get serious with anyone."

"I'm not gonna fuck Holly over. I wouldn't do that."

"What, you're in love with her?"

His words dripped with sarcasm, and I almost flinched. He had every right to assume I wanted nothing more than some fun between the sheets. Don't get me wrong, I absolutely wanted to lose myself in Holly again and again and again, but there was a hell of a lot more than that when it came to how I felt about Holly.

"I don't know if I'm ready to say that, but I'd like a chance to see what happens."

"Fuck," Alex repeated, spinning away from me and striding toward the closest plane to kick his boot against the tire. "Does she know this?"

"I've tried to make it clear, but I'm not sure what she wants."

Alex circled back, striding right up to me. "Do *not* fuck her over. I will kick your ass."

"I know," I said, trying to keep my calm. It wasn't that I didn't expect this from Alex, but it chafed to be faced with his assumptions. "I promise you, this isn't just a fling to me."

Alex stepped back, rolling his head from side to side as if to ease the tension in his neck and shoulders. When he looked back to me, he shook his head slowly. "I knew you had a thing for her back in high school. I guess I figured you'd moved on."

"I did, and I didn't."

Alex stared at me, his gaze considering. After a long silence, a heavy one at that, he shook his head again. "You mean to tell me you've had a thing for my twin sister for fucking *years?*"

Leaning my head back, I stared up at the corrugated metal roof above, my eyes tracing the lines of the steel beams. Leveling my gaze with Alex again, I shrugged. "I don't know how to describe it. Before you go thinking I was sitting around pining for her, that's not what it was. So yeah, I had a thing for her in high school, but..."

My words trailed off because I didn't quite know how to explain the rest. I wasn't about to tell Alex that Holly had been the main star in most of my fantasies since high school. I wouldn't say I had been hung up on her, more that I once had a thing for her, a pretty messy event got in the way, and I moved on. Now... well, now things were different.

Alex picked up the thread for me. "Life got in the way, in a big way. That accident hit a lot of us hard. Not that you're asking, but Holly was never in love with Jake. Mostly, they started dating because Caleb and Ella were together all the damn time." Alex looked away, taking a deep breath and bouncing his heel against the plane tire behind him.

When he looked back, his gaze was dead serious. "Look, Holly would kick my fucking ass if I tried to pull the whole overprotective brother shit on her, so I'm not going to interfere. Unless..." He paused, lifting a finger and pointing it straight at me. "Unless you fuck her over. Obviously, I would tell any friend of ours that if they were looking for something serious with you, they needed to look in a different direction. If this is what Holly wants, it's her business, but don't fuck with her."

My heart gave a hard thump, rattling against my ribs. I wasn't about to tell Alex the depth of my feelings for her, not just yet. I wasn't so sure what she wanted.

I held his gaze and nodded slowly. "I get it, but you don't have to worry."

Alex shook his head. "Are you going to tell her that I know?"

"Yeah. I'm not stupid enough to try to keep it a secret."

Alex's smile was genuine this time. "Oh yeah, because that would definitely be fucking stupid. Anyway, let's take a look at this," he said, turning to get to work.

Alex quickly opened up the compartment over the plane's engine. The plane wasn't mine but belonged to a good friend who was out of town. He'd asked me to set it up for Alex to take a look at it since Alex was a certified aviation mechanic.

We managed to move past that awkward conversation and got to work. As we were leaving a few hours later, Alex glanced over when we paused between our trucks. "So, tell me, is Holly the reason you haven't dated anyone as far as I know since last fall or thereabouts?"

Jesus fucking Christ. I wasn't about to tell Alex the details of our few brief minutes prior to recent events. He didn't need to know I'd almost fucked his sister in a closet and then in a dressing room at a fundraiser. I was in a bit of a bind. He wasn't my best friend for nothing. He knew me well. Catching his gaze, I shrugged, apparently my go-to response when it came to trying to talk about Holly.

"Not exactly."

I stayed as vague as possible. But there was no way in hell I could tell him how embedded Holly was in my thoughts.

He chuckled before he turned away. "Don't forget what I said."

I stood there in the cold, the sound of a raven's call sharp in the sky as it flew above, then my boots crunching on the snow in the parking lot as I turned to walk around my truck and climb in.

Chapter Twenty-One

HOLLY

After walking into the break room, I sank into a chair with a sigh. "Fuck, I'm tired," I said, reaching up to tighten my ponytail as I cast a wan smile toward Chris, who was sitting on the other side of the small round table.

Chris nodded with me, running a hand through his hair and sipping his coffee. "Coffee's fresh and strong as hell if you want some. I'm too tired to stand up and get it for you."

I laughed as I stood and crossed over to the counter along the wall. "I need the caffeine bad enough to get my ass over here."

After pouring a cup, I added a dash of cream and sat down across from him again. My shift was over as of five minutes earlier. The ER had been busy all afternoon. There had been two car accidents on the highway outside of Willow Brook. It was icy out today, with just enough sunshine to melt the snow and give the roads a sheen of slickness. We'd have black ice once darkness fell tonight.

"We were lucky. No one died," I commented.

Chris took another slow sip of coffee and nodded. We sat in companionable silence for a few minutes, each of us nursing our coffee and letting the adrenaline drain from our systems. When you handled emergency room work, you needed your adrenaline to get through it, to keep you focused, sharp, and on top of it. On long days, once it was over, it was a relief to unwind. Sometimes it took hours. After the day I had, I knew I'd be wired tonight, probably for a few hours after I got home.

"So, tell me something good. Any updates on Nate? Or your virginity?"

Although Chris was teasing, he didn't get under my skin. We had that kind of friendship where we could tease about sensitive subjects because we both knew that the other one understood.

"Well, I managed to lose my virginity," I offered with a wink.

"You go, girl," he said with a wide grin. "Was it awful? As a man, I have no perspective on this."

I burst out laughing. "I would imagine not. I think it's probably different for you. But no, it wasn't awful." I felt my cheeks getting hot because it had been the opposite of awful. It had been amazing.

Chris arched a brow. "It looks like it wasn't awful at all. So, what now?"

I took a long swallow of my coffee, savoring the flavor and the kick of caffeine my system craved. "I don't know." I set my cup down. Simply speaking of it tightened my chest and sent anxiety spiraling through me.

Nate was confusing me because it seemed as if he wanted me to take this seriously. I didn't think he understood. Ever since my body had awoken to Nate, I was fairly certain he'd ruined me for anyone else. Though I would forever be glad I lost my virginity to him and not someone else, I was terrified of how I felt.

Lord knows what emotions fled across my face, but Chris reached across the table. "Oh hon, you really like him."

Emotion tightened my throat and tears pricked hot at

the backs of my eyes. Giving his hand a squeeze, I snagged a tissue from the box sitting in the middle of the table. "Yeah. I guess so, but it's stupid. I can't"—I paused to blow my nose—"I can't let myself fall for him."

"Well, you wouldn't be the first pair of friends to fall in love."

"Oh my God, it's not... We're not in love."

Chris's warm gaze held mine, completely serious. "I always thought Nate liked you. Maybe you should just play things by ear."

"Well, I already am, so..." I shrugged, swiping at my tears.

He drained his coffee and eyed me. "Maybe something will come of it," he finally said. "But nothing will if you don't give it a chance."

I drained my own coffee. "I know."

Standing, he strode around the table and tugged me into a quick hug. A sly grin curled his lips as he stepped back. "At least you got rid of that pesky virginity. I'm guessing it was awesome."

Chris always knew just when it was time to shift from serious to funny. I nudged him with my shoulder. "See you later this week."

"Gotcha," he called as we walked out together, turning in opposite directions.

I hurried back to the nurse's station to quickly take care of some last-minute charting for the night. Within a few minutes, I was done for the evening, and the last nurse to leave from the day shift. The evening crew was in full swing now, the hustle and bustle following me down the hallway as I left.

It wasn't fully dark yet when I got outside. Streaks of lavender and pink lingered in the wispy gray sky. The bracing air hit me, giving me a jolt. When I reached my car, I was surprised to see it hadn't started. I must've forgotten to use my remote start.

Climbing into my little hatchback, I pressed the start button and got nothing but a clicking sound. I pressed it again. A few more clicks came back to me.

"Fuck. Probably a dead battery," I muttered to myself.

Glancing around the parking lot, I saw there was no one around. My head fell back against the headrest, as I mentally prepared myself to go back inside and sweet-talk someone into coming out to help me jumpstart my car.

Climbing back out, I tugged my coat tighter around me and started walking through the parking lot when a pair of headlights illuminated me. Glancing to the side, I recognized Nate's truck. I couldn't help the curl of anticipation that spun through me. I had more important things on my mind, though—namely, for him to help me jumpstart my car.

Stepping to the side, I let him pass where he came to a stop, his window rolling down. "I was just coming to see what you were up to tonight," he said by way of greeting.

"What I'm up to right now is I need someone to jumpstart my car, and I think you're the guy," I replied with a grin.

His eyes crinkled at the corners with his return smile. "Of course I can. Where are you parked?"

I pointed to where my car was on the far side of the parking lot. "Hop in," he said, nodding his head toward the passenger door.

I was just cold enough to want a short ride across the parking lot. Jogging around the truck, I hopped in. Of course, Nate had reached across to open the door for me.

"Oh God, it's so warm in here." I sighed, hugging my waist and shivering slightly.

Nate's dark eyes cut to me as he chuckled. Oh geez. I had practical matters on my mind—my car that wouldn't start—and still, at the look in his eyes, my body revved. Oh my.

Within seconds, he had stopped in front of my car, and we climbed out together. I popped the hood of my car while he got his jumper cables out. Once he had the two vehicles hooked up, he nodded. "Start her up."

I hit my start button repeatedly once I was in the car.

"Nothing's happening," I called, because I liked to state the obvious sometimes.

Nate came over to the driver's side where I had the door propped open. Resting one of his hands on the roof, he leaned in. "Nothing?"

"Nope." I pressed the start button a few more times. My car obediently made a clicking sound, yet the engine didn't start.

When I looked up, his mouth was right there. I moved on instinct, not even thinking about it. Leaning up, I slid my hand around his nape, closing the distance between us and bringing my lips against his.

When I felt his muffled laugh, a sense of joy spun inside my chest. I might have startled him, but he got with the program right away. His tongue slipped inside to tease along mine, and he threaded his hand in my hair, deepening our kiss.

By the time he drew back, I was on fire, gasping and wishing we were anywhere other than a public parking lot at work on an icy cold, winter evening.

"I'll take you home. Or you can come to my place. Take your pick," he said.

My lower belly clenched at the sound of his voice. Sanity was not my friend today. In fact, sanity and reason had fled the vicinity.

"Your place."

Why I chose his place, I didn't know. Perhaps my tiny, drowned out voice of reason was trying to make sure he didn't spend too much time at my place, to protect it from being forever colored by memories of him.

"Come on. You can have Alex come out and take a look at your car tomorrow," he replied.

With his hand warm around mine, I followed him back

to his truck. Once we were inside and Nate had started to drive out, I commented, "If I ask Alex to come take a look at it, then he'll ask how I got home from work."

Nate rolled to a stop in the middle of the driveway out of the hospital, his eyes sliding to mine. "Right. I'm sure you can just tell him you caught a ride with a friend."

I didn't like the look in his eyes. I didn't know what I saw, but it was something. "Please don't tell me you told Alex about us."

Nate leaned his head back with a sigh. "He asked me. After he saw me kiss you in the parking lot."

Frustration and annoyance swirled inside me. "What did you tell him?"

"Not much, certainly not any of the details. I got a lecture, and he threatened to kick my ass if I hurt you."

Nate's gaze was somber. My heart was fluttering rapidly in my chest. Between my desire and the mix of emotions about Nate, about us, I was all tangled up inside. My twin brother was way too damn nosy sometimes.

Nate clearly sensed the potential for my anger and tried to head me off. "Look, he's my best friend. There's no real way for me to hide this from him for too long. I told him the truth, that I wanted a shot with you. That's it."

"That's what you told him?" I asked, disbelief coloring my tone.

"Yeah, that's what I told him. Because that's the truth."

"Since when did you want anything more than friends with benefits? With anyone?"

"Since you," he said flatly, his eyes almost daring me to argue the point.

My mouth must've fallen open, which I only noticed when he reached out and tapped his finger under my chin, a sly smile curling his lips. Flustered, I snapped my mouth shut and looked away, taking a shaky breath.

This was everything I wanted, and yet I didn't trust it. Although I had walked straight through the fire of the crushing pain of that car accident back in high school, when my best friend almost died and another dear friend actually did, one thing I had never quite shaken was the blunt reality that you learned when something like that happened. Life can change in a blinding flash.

Ever since then, it had been hard for me to hang my hopes onto anything, to have faith in anything. Much less, to believe Nate had suddenly changed his colors.

For years, he'd excelled at playing casual. There was never any confusion on anyone's behalf about what he wanted—sex and fun. I was long past that. I wanted the fairytale, while the part of me that had held myself strong all these years scoffed at the very idea. I was a little conflicted, you might say.

The heat coming from the vents in his truck was the only sound. The sky had lost its last glimmers of color, stars in the deepening darkness glittered above the jagged peaks of the mountains, a dark silhouette against the horizon.

I finally turned back to look at Nate because I was starting to feel like a bit of a coward. His dark brown gaze held mine, steady and unwavering. I didn't know what to do with any of this. Nate had always been the tease, the joker, the counterpoint to his more serious older brother.

Annoyance flashed, and I grabbed onto it. I suddenly recalled how this entire train of conversation started. "I can't believe you said anything to Alex," I muttered.

Nate's eyes narrowed. "And what the hell was I supposed to say?"

"Well, you didn't have to kiss me," I protested.

"Since when did you become a coward?"

Oh, hell no.

"I'm not a fucking coward, how dare you say that?" I retorted, my words sounding stronger than I actually felt.

Chapter Twenty-Two

HOLLY

Nate cocked his head to the side, arching a brow. As he looked at me, his eyes darkened, beckoning a response from my body. I hated how easily he affected me. Nothing but a look from him could coax the need to kindle inside of me. It was always waiting—a hot burning coal, waiting to be set aflame with a spark.

I didn't want to think about anything. Not how fast I was falling for him, not how his sudden interest in something other than casual sex was confusing me, not how much it meant that I had lost my virginity to him, none of it. It felt as if a bolt of lightning snapped through the air on the heels of a rumble of thunder. I might not be able to make any sense of my feelings, but I could lose myself in him, in this wild need that exploded like fireworks between us.

I leaned across the console, pausing, my lips perhaps an inch from his. "Don't you dare call me a coward."

Nate was quiet, with the air heavy between us. Then, our lips met in a hot, wild, messy kiss. In a matter of seconds, desire took over—strong and elemental, so powerful we practically created our own weather system when we touched. It wouldn't have surprised me if sparks flew from our lips at the point of joining.

I was burning up inside. I needed him inside of me. Now.

I was jolted out of the madness when there was a sharp knock on the driver's side window. We broke apart, both of us breathing heavily.

"Fuck," I muttered.

Nate laughed softly, which only served to notch up my lingering anger from his comment about me being a coward. My anger only fueled my need. When he glanced out the window, shifting in his seat, I noticed it was Dan, one of the nursing assistants at the hospital. I didn't know him particularly well, but still.

Gossip was like blood in the water in Willow Brook, especially in the middle of the winter. Everyone was bored and restless, and there were no tourists for distraction. I doubted it was possible that the guy didn't notice we were kissing, although perhaps the misty windows would save me.

Nate rolled down his window. "Yeah?" he asked.

"Just letting you know you're blocking the drive to the ER. We have an ambulance on the way in a few minutes," Dan replied.

Before I even thought about it, I was leaning around Nate and asking, "Anything serious?"

Dan's eyes widened when he saw me. "Someone with chest pains. You're done for the night. Go home. Everything okay with your car, by the way?" he asked.

"Dead battery. Nate's giving me a ride."

"Gotcha. Well, I'm sure I'll see you on shift soon," he said. He stepped back with a wave as the sound of a siren became audible in the distance.

Nate rolled his window up and began driving. Neither one of us spoke for a few moments, while I contemplated whether or not I had just been seen making out with Nate by one of my co-workers in a fucking truck in the parking lot at work.

My cheeks were hot at nothing more than the idea of that kind of gossip, not to mention that my baseline state was hot and bothered whenever I was anywhere near Nate.

"Where to?" he asked again, as if I might have changed my mind.

For a flash, I contemplated telling him to drop me off at home and shooing him away. The problem was, I wanted him too damn much. My panties were wet, my nipples were so tight they ached, and the hum of desire permeated every cell of my body. I was practically vibrating.

"Your place." He had stopped at the end of the drive that led to the hospital. When I looked toward him, the feel of his gaze alone sent a hot shiver through me. "Well, get on with it," I muttered.

His laugh was low and gruff, sending goose bumps chasing over the surface of my skin.

Nate lived just a few minutes past downtown Willow Brook. I knew from Alex that Nate had mostly built this place himself with a little help from his older brother, Caleb, and their father. I hadn't been here in a while, but it was just as I recalled.

He lived in a timber frame style home. Although it was dark out, I knew there was a view of a field with the mountains in the backdrop. The same stream that ran through the back of my parents' property was running through his. I'd grown up just down the road, a few miles away as the crow flew. Nate's parents lived next door to mine, that proximity the seed that planted his lifelong friendship with my brother.

We parked in the back of the home, walking onto the small deck that had an entrance into the kitchen. Stepping inside, we knocked the snow off our boots on the soft gray tile. The kitchen had a counter running against the back wall, along with the refrigerator toward one side, and the oven and stove flanking it. Directly opposite that was an oval-shaped island. Countertops of soft gray granite matched the floor. Pots and pans hung above the island from a decorative rack. Just beyond the island, hardwood floor demarcated the kitchen from the open style living room and sitting area.

I looked over to the far corner, where a woodstove was situated with seating around it. On the other side, a flat screen television was mounted on the wall. A sectional couch smack in the middle of the room was angled such that you could see the television, along with the view out to the front of the home. Like so many homes in Alaska, there were windows floor to ceiling to take full advantage of the spectacular view.

The upstairs was only on the back half of the house with a set of stairs to the side leading to a balcony with a railing so the view could be seen from the second floor. Just now, it occurred to me that I'd never actually been in the upstairs of Nate's home. He'd built the home about five years ago after he got his pilot's license. Although I'd been here, I'd never had reason to go upstairs, and I presumed the bedrooms were up there.

Nate occasionally had casual gatherings, which of course meant my brother was invited, and me, by extension. Suddenly, the weight of everything that was happening between us slammed into me. I didn't want to think right now, not at all.

Turning, I kicked my boots off as Nate stepped back out onto the deck to sprinkle salt and sand on the icy surface. Were this any other man, I would have felt a sense of tension, perhaps unfamiliarity from being in their space. With Nate, I was experiencing an odd combination of familiarity and newness. The sands had shifted beneath our friendship. About the only time I wasn't running laps in my thoughts, occasionally tripping and stumbling, we were tangled up together—the fierce, white-hot desire burning between us sending my worries up in smoke.

Hanging my jacket on a coat stand beside the door, I glanced up when he came back through the door, a gust of cold air following him. My nipples perked up in response as the cold air filtered through the fabric of my shirt. I was dressed about as un-sexily as possible. I had on a pair of bright purple scrubs tonight, the color cheery for me when I was at the hospital for a long day. I preferred to wear loose scrubs when I worked because I needed to be comfortable.

This was quite the opposite of what I'd been wearing that fateful evening at the fundraiser last fall. Taking a shaky breath, I willed myself to stay calm. Yet, desire was beating like a drum in my body, liquid need spinning through my veins and whispering there was only one relief.

Nate tossed an empty plastic cup into the bucket of salt and sand mix by the door before sliding the lid back over it. After toeing his boots off and shrugging out of his jacket, he turned to face me.

My eyes—my naughty, willful eyes—tracked up and down his body, absorbing the sight of him. He smelled like cool winter air with a hint of wood smoke clinging to him. He wore jeans, faded and soft, the muscles of his thighs filling them. My eyes tracked their way up, his cotton jersey doing little to hide his muscled chest and shoulders. It hadn't skipped my notice that his arousal was evident.

A flash of relief pierced me. At least I wasn't alone in this wild rush. Restlessness nudged me. I needed to move, needed to do something with the tornado of emotion and desire spinning wildly inside. My thoughts jostled inside my brain, competing for attention and space, crowded out by pure lust.

Stepping to Nate, I boldly slid my hand over the hard ridge of his arousal, leaning up to catch his lips in a kiss. I startled him, his breath coming out in a low groan against my lips. Drawing back quickly, I made quick work of his fly, sliding my hand into his briefs and freeing his cock. The velvety skin was hot, a drop of pre-cum rolling off the tip when I glanced down.

Shoving him against the door, I shimmied down, swiping that drop up with my tongue. Satisfaction raced through me when he murmured my name roughly, his hand lacing into my hair tightly. I was no blowjob virgin and settled in to drive him as wild as he drove me. Dragging my tongue along the underside, I swirled it around the broad head of his cock, savoring the salty tang of pre-cum and taking him into my mouth, all the way to the base, licking, stroking, and sucking.

It wasn't as if I had any doubts that Nate was well-endowed, but this was the first time I'd gotten this up close and personal. He was long, thick and hard, reminding me precisely why I was still a little sore from the other night. I heard his head thump against the wall, as I slid my hand up and down in time with the motion of my mouth.

Another drop of pre-cum danced across my tongue. "Holly," he murmured gruffly.

His hand tightened in my hair, the sting on my scalp welcome as sensation collided with the need churning inside of me. I drew back, slowly dragging my tongue around the tip. With a muttered growl, he tried to yank me up, but I wasn't having it. Driven to make him crazy, I drew back slowly before taking him in deeply until the head of his cock bumped the back of my throat. Another slide along the length of him, and I felt the pulse of his cock, savoring the rough cry of my name from his throat as he found his release.

I waited for a few beats before slowly easing back with a last swipe of my tongue. As I straightened, I opened my eyes, taking him in. Leaning against the door, he was so damn sexy, my breath caught in my throat. My fierce desire surged. With his jeans hanging open and his shirt loose, his eyes were at half-mast, his gaze intense. The brief surge of power I felt at having him at my mercy dissipated at the heated look in his eyes.

This man. Only this man could melt me with nothing more than a look.

With his dark gaze locked to mine, he kicked his foot against the door, pushing away. In a flash, he was lifting me against him, not even bothering to deal with his clothes. My legs curled reflexively around his hips and a gasp escaped when he nipped at my neck. Heat shot through me. He didn't hesitate, moving swiftly across the living room and up the stairs, carrying me easily in his arms. His hold was strong, the kind that made me feel safe—as if he'd always have me. I suppose he would. In more ways than one.

Restless with need driving me as he carried me up the stairs, I dusted kisses along his neck, savoring the salty tang of his skin and the rapid beat of his pulse. Then, he was shouldering through a door in the center of the balcony upstairs. With a nudge of his elbow on the light switch by the door, two lamps in the corners came on, the lights casting a soft glow in the room.

I barely had time to absorb his bedroom—a large king-size bed in the center of the room, low to the floor with built-in bookshelves framing it on either side, and a dresser under a side window were the only furnishings.

Nate practically tossed me on the bed, his gaze dark as he looked down at me. "I need you," he said bluntly, those three words making my sex clench.

Our remaining clothes came off in a tangle. The next thing I knew, the mattress dipped, his knee pressing down between my thighs. My nipples were tight, my lower belly clenching, and I was wet, so wet, I could hardly bear it.

His gaze swept down my body, the heat of it making my skin prickle. When his eyes traveled back up to meet mine, a wicked gleam entered his gaze.

"Your turn."

Chapter Twenty-Three

NATE

Holly's skin glistened in the soft glow cast from the lamps on either side of the bed. Her nipples were tight and dusky pink, her breasts plump and full. A bolt of lust shot through me. My body had all but forgotten she'd just brought me to release in her mouth. My cock was already swollen and aching again. I was barely clinging to my control, but I would wait. I needed to savor this, savor her.

Leaning back slightly, I skimmed my fingertips on the insides of her thighs, watching as her lips parted on a gasp and she shifted restlessly. Her tongue swiped across her bottom lip, her gaze holding mine.

That was one thing I loved about Holly. She didn't hesitate, never once shying away from looking at me. Just now, it occurred to me that I'd been the only man to have her like this. I'd never considered myself a possessive man, it wasn't particularly my nature.

Holly proved me wrong on that point. At the idea that no man had ever been inside of her other than me, the surge of possessiveness and raw need was fierce. I couldn't even countenance another man being like this with her. Skimming my fingers higher, I dragged the backs of my knuckles across her lower belly as she rippled under my touch.

Cupping one of her breasts in my palm, I savored the weight, the feel of her silky skin, and the way her nipple peaked tighter when I brushed my thumb across it and pinched it lightly between my thumb and forefinger. I couldn't hold back anymore, bending forward to catch her other nipple with my mouth, swirling my tongue around it, and sucking it lightly before nipping it with my teeth.

She was so responsive, flexing up into me, her hand burying in my hair and gripping as she arched up. I knew if I eased my hips down against her right now, that would be it. The need to bury myself in her slick heat would override everything else.

Holding back, I swirled my tongue around her nipple, my hands mapping my way down her body, dusting kisses over the soft curve of her belly and pushing her thighs apart. On a muttered gasp, she fell back against the pillows. Lifting my head, I glanced up. Her breath came in ragged pants, her breasts rising and falling rapidly. Her long blonde hair was in a tangle on the pillows, and her cheeks were flushed.

She was so fucking beautiful and so sexy, she took my breath away. I let my eyes slide down. The core of her was pink, wet, and glistening. I trailed my fingers over her slick folds, watching as her hips rose into my touch.

"Tell me what you want," I murmured, watching her face.

Her eyes dragged open, her gaze dark and fiery.

"More of this?" I asked with a tease of my fingers just over her entrance.

"Nate!" she said on a gasp as I sank one finger inside of her.

I meant to tease her more, but as usual, I loved watching her go wild. When her hips rose to meet a stroke of my finger, another finger joined the first. I brought my mouth to her, growling in satisfaction when she cried out, her hips bucking up against my tongue when I swirled it around her clit and buried my fingers inside of her.

She was close to the edge already. I could feel the quickening with every stroke of my fingers. I drank her in, her juices slick on my hand and against my mouth. Another few strokes, and then her cry was sharp as she shuddered against me. Her entire body rippled as her channel clamped down around my fingers. I drew back slowly, almost reluctant to leave the taste of her. Overriding that desire was the need to be buried deeply inside of her.

Rising up, I paused, my cock swelling when I looked down at her. With her skin flushed with passion, her pupils dark and dilated when she dragged her eyes open, my heart squeezed like a fist in my chest, setting to beat so hard and fast I could barely think or hear over the emotion rushing through me.

I knew when this began that Holly was far more to me than any woman had ever been. And yet, I hadn't been prepared for this piercing connection to her. The depth and sweetness of it was an ache in the center of my heart.

I couldn't have known that giving in to the desire between us would only serve to spin me into the flame that would burn me to ashes if I couldn't have her—on every level, body, heart, and soul. Completely.

She shifted her legs, reaching up, her fingers skimming over my chest. That subtle touch was a lash across my skin, slivers of fire chasing in its wake. Fisting my cock, I dragged the head of it through her folds, clinging to my control when she gasped, her body still shuddering from the echoes of her climax.

In one swift thrust, I filled her, her slick core drawing me in and clenching around me. Leaning forward slowly, I eased over her, groaning at the feel of her damp, silky skin against mine, her softness to my hardness.

Just as I settled against her, awareness sliced through me,

and I started to move back, not fast enough though. She curled her legs around me and held me in place.

"Where are you going?" she demanded, her voice husky and bossy as hell.

God. I fucking loved this woman.

"Condom," I grunted.

"Didn't we already have this conversation?" she murmured. "I get the shot. I'm a nurse, for crying out loud. I'm clean as a fucking whistle. And I trust you because you're a freaking Boy Scout," she said with a sly grin.

Seeing as I was already buried in the silken core of her, the last thing I wanted to do was pull out and put a barrier between us. But this was her call. "Are you sure?" I asked, watching her eyes.

They widened, flashing with annoyance. "Oh my God, yes!"

I didn't need any further instruction, not when her hips arched up into mine, beckoning me and urging me on. Dipping my head, I caught her lips in a kiss as I drew back and filled her again.

I felt like a fucking teenager. I should've been sated, way back when she drove me wild with her mouth. But no, I was already racing off to another climax, my balls tightening and heat twisting at the base of my spine. She gasped into my mouth as I surged inside of her again, tearing her lips free with a ragged cry.

My hips drummed into hers, damp, slick sounds from our skin colliding with every stroke. I felt her pussy throb and clench around me before her entire body shuddered again, my name a husky shout. I tumbled over the edge with her, my release like the force of thunder snapping through my body. I fell against her, quickly rolling to the side and taking her with me.

She was relaxed and soft against me, little ripples from her climax passing through her body, her core squeezing my cock gently. I felt as if I'd been hit by a truck, slammed to the ground with a force of pleasure so intense I was wiped out.

We laid there in a tangle of limbs, the sounds of our breath filling the air. Thought slowly filtered back online in my brain. I didn't want Holly to ever move away from me. We could just stay right here in my bed and do that about a thousand times. Maybe, just maybe, that would be enough to take the edge off my burning need for her.

After a few moments, I felt her shift. Opening my eyes, I caught her gaze when she lifted her head and rested her chin on my chest. Her eyes searched mine, and my heart set to thudding against my ribs again. I didn't know what I meant to Holly, yet I knew what she meant to me. She had slayed me, completely ruined me for any other woman. I needed to do whatever it took to get her on the same page.

"Thanks for the ride," she said, her mouth curling at the corners with a grin.

For a moment, I was confused, but then I remembered. It said something that I had no idea how long we'd been here since we'd been unable to start her car.

"Anytime," I replied.

———

I woke in the darkness with Holly warm and soft beside me. I was curled up behind her, holding her pressed against my morning arousal. I didn't bother to think, my body simply acted. Sliding my hand over the soft curve of her belly and teasing my fingers between her thighs, I found her hot, wet, and ready. She murmured my name, the sound an erotic jolt to my system. Lifting her leg slightly, I sank home inside of her. It was a brief interlude, a slow, sensual fuck in the darkness.

The last thing I remembered was falling asleep still buried inside of her just after she had rolled her head to the

side to dust kisses along my jawline. When I woke later, the
sheets were cool, and Holly was gone.

I had never panicked in my life about a woman being
gone in the morning. But right now, I panicked. Kicking the
covers off, I scrambled out of bed. After I stumbled into a
pair of boxers and walked into the kitchen, I found a note
beside the coffee pot. The coffee was still warm, letting me
know it hadn't been too long since she'd left.

*Nate, thanks again for the ride last night. I got called into an
emergency shift. A friend from work picked me up. I'm sure I'll see
you soon.*

Holly

I didn't know what it was about that damn note, but
somehow, I knew that Holly intended to create some
distance between us. I didn't like it, not at all.

Chapter Twenty-Four

HOLLY

"Oh my God! You have got to be kidding me," I said, leaning around Charlie to look at Jesse.

Jesse shrugged, and rolled his eyes. "Definitely not kidding."

"I swear, someday, she's really going to hurt herself if she keeps trying to do that," I added.

"You're telling me," Charlie chimed in. "I mean, I worry about my mom but she's living with us. With Carrie, she insists on living on her own. I guess she's perfectly okay, but now she's chasing around trees for that new kitten."

"Yeah, that kitten likes to climb trees higher than old Herman," Beck Steele said from beside his wife Maisie, where they sat across the table. Beck was another hotshot firefighter, and Maisie was the main dispatcher for Willow Brook. She'd stolen Beck's heart a while back and now they had two toddlers.

I took a sip of my drink. Normally, I went for beer or wine, but tonight the bar was having a special on margaritas. Ella laughed beside me. Glancing to her, I was about to ask her something when I heard Nate's voice. I reflexively turned in the direction of his voice, only to whip my head back when Ella muttered something under her breath.

Even though I didn't hear what she said, I hadn't been her best friend since kindergarten for nothing. I knew she was teasing me. "What?"

Fortunately, everyone else around us was occupied with other topics, whether it was Carrie's old cat, Herman, or her new kitten, or the weather and other sundry matters.

"I said somebody is pretty tuned in tonight. He's halfway across the bar, for God's sake," Ella explained.

I took another sip of my margarita and rolled my eyes, feeling my cheeks heat and relieved for the dim lighting at Wildlands. We were having dinner and drinks, nothing unusual. Charlie and Jessie were here, along with Maisie and Beck, and Ella and Caleb. This wasn't the first time I was acutely aware of my single state.

I was quite relieved Rachel Garrett was on the way to meet us. Rachel was a medical assistant at Willow Brook Family Medicine. She was a friend, and she was also single. It was nice not to feel so alone in my state. Nate—and, oh hell, my brother—approached our table with Remy Martin. Remy was a recent transplant to Willow Brook, having taken a position on one of the hotshot crews here. He was a southern boy from Louisiana. He had moved up here after a stint on a hotshot crew in Washington State in the mountains, which meant he had actually survived winter before.

Looking up, the moment my eyes landed on Nate's, my lower belly clenched, and that oh-so-familiar heat radiated from my core, blooming through my entire body. I forced my gaze from Nate. The last thing I needed was to get all hot and bothered over him with my brother right here. Somehow, I had avoided hearing any commentary from Alex about Nate. It still smarted that he had seen Nate kiss me.

When I looked away from Nate, my eyes landed on Remy. I willed my body to notice just how sexy Remy was. Because good Lord, that man had it going on—hair the color of rich amber, with green eyes to go along with it. It was impossible for a hotshot firefighter not to be in amazing physical condition, and Remy fit the bill—all rugged strength, he moved with a graceful agility. He had a slight teasing grin and a sexy southern accent paired with it. In short, he was hot as hell.

I could notice all of that, objectively speaking, yet I felt absolutely nothing when I looked at him. He might as well have been my brother. Dammit.

It had been three full days since I'd woken up in Nate's bed and fled the scene. Instead of taking a few days off, I signed up to cover some extra shifts when I heard two nurses were out sick. I'd been working like crazy and was exhausted, but I had a quick answer for why I hadn't seen Nate. I was working.

Those of us already seated shuffled around, making room at the massive round table we had snagged in the far corner. Conveniently, Remy snagged the open chair beside me before Nate could, who ended up at an angle across from me. There would be no sneaky teasing me with touches. I was both relieved and let down. Sigh.

"Hey, Holl," Alex called from across the table when he slipped into a chair beside Nate.

I lifted my fingers in a wave and flashed a tight smile. "Hey guys, how's it going?"

"Haven't seen you in days," Nate replied pointedly, his eyes lingering a little too long on me for my comfort with this crowd.

Alex's gaze flicked from Nate to me, far too perceptive and knowing. None of this was comfortable for me. Blessedly, Beck said something to Nate, tugging him into a conversation and allowing me to nurse my margarita, and do my best to ignore him.

"How's it going, darlin'?" Remy asked politely from my side.

Oh, and Remy dropped endearments all the time. It was

quite sweet and added to his sexy quotient. Still, not even a *zing* of attraction for me.

Glancing up, I again attempted to elicit some sort of chemistry beyond my objective appreciation of his beauty. Nothing, absolutely nothing. I smiled up at him. "I'm doing fine. How are you adjusting to Willow Brook? This is your first winter here, right?" I asked.

"Yes, ma'am," he said. "I love it. I love snow, probably because I never even saw it until I moved away from where I grew up. This is my first winter here, but I went through winter in the mountains in Washington, so it's not like I wasn't prepared. It's a little darker here, and a bit colder, but I can handle it."

Rachel showed up just at that moment, replying to Remy as she slipped into a chair beside him. "Are you sure?"

Remy glanced to her. "Yes, darlin'. I'm sure. I've never had trouble staying warm," he drawled.

I happened to be looking right at Rachel and noticed her cheeks flush. *Well, hmm.*

I suppose it was convenient that Remy didn't rev my engine because he clearly revved Rachel's. Conversation carried on around me and the night went on as usual. The only fly in the ointment, so to speak, was the occasional glance from Nate.

I overheard Alex asking him something and couldn't help my ears from perking up. "What time do you leave for your weekend trip?"

"Tomorrow," Nate replied.

Right about then, a woman approached the table, calling Nate's name. Looking beyond Nate, I took in the woman. There was a flirtatious smile on her face and her long dark hair swung around her shoulders. She stopped right behind him, resting her hand on his shoulder.

I didn't doubt, not for one second, that whoever the hell this woman was, she and Nate had likely had a fling. She was quite beautiful, tall, and leggy. Of course, certainly not as curvy as me. She was the kind of woman who, on a bad day, made me feel a little insecure.

Just now, after three days of successfully avoiding Nate, her presence and teasing approach were the equivalent of a swinging hammer into the coffin of my poorly decided choice to let myself get involved with him in any way, shape, or form.

I could see Nate's eyes widen slightly in surprise. "Oh, hey, Brenda," he said easily. "I didn't know you were in town."

My eyes flicked down as her hand squeezed his shoulder, sliding down over his arm. I knew far better than I wished just how good Nate's muscled shoulders felt. I took a shaky breath, willing the jealousy spiking through me to disappear. I had no right to be jealous. I was being crazy.

"You didn't realize I was with the party you're flying out to the lodge?" Brenda asked.

Nate shook his head, a hint of tension crossing his features. If I didn't know him so well, I wouldn't have noticed. But I knew him, quite well.

"Nope, missed that detail. I didn't get a list of everybody going, just how many and my main contact."

Brenda laughed lightly, her hand still resting on his shoulder. "Well, it ought to be a great trip. I sure hope you'll be staying for the weekend as well."

I could feel Ella's gaze on me from the side, and abruptly decided it was not in my best interest to remain here for this little display. I now knew what Nate would be doing this weekend. Or rather, who.

"I need to get going," I said, my voice low as I leaned toward Ella.

Her green gaze met mine, concern shimmering in the depths. "Are you sure?" she asked.

"Of course," I replied quickly, not caring to wait. I gulped down the last of my margarita and stood, quickly gathering my coat and purse before hurrying out with a general wave at the table.

I saw Nate look in my direction, but Brenda was still talking with him. I hurried home, almost running along the sidewalk. A light snow was falling in the darkness, the half moon blurred by the clouds and the snow.

Within minutes, I shut the door to my apartment, locking it and leaning against it with a deep breath. Hot tears rolled down my cheeks. I had screwed up. This was epically bad.

I knew I needed to create some distance between Nate and me. I had intellectually known he would likely move on. Yet, I hadn't quite been prepared for what it would feel like to watch it play out right in front of my eyes.

Pushing away from the door, I knuckled my tears away and shrugged out of my jacket. Padding across the living room, I turned up the heat and set the kettle on to boil. I needed tea. It was either that, or drink an entire bottle of wine by myself to try to forget everything that had passed between Nate and me.

Just after I turned the burner on under the kettle and was walking toward the bathroom to start the water, there was a sharp knock at my door. My heart started pounding. Part of me was insanely hopeful that Nate was here to declare his love for me. Yet, the other part of me knew I had to face down my fears and tell him the plain truth. This thing with us had to stop. *Now.*

Although I was a mess inside, I latched onto the anger and jealousy that was burning through me. That was what would power me through this. I walked to the door, swinging it open.

Nate stood there, his cheeks ruddy from the cold and his eyes boring into mine. "Why have you been avoiding me?" he demanded.

"Because, this"—I paused, waving my hand back and forth between us—"has to stop. You go have your weekend with Brenda. Don't let me get in the way. Don't think anything is ever going to happen with me again."

I was furious, emotion and tears tightening in my chest and throat, but I wasn't about to break down in front of Nate. I had too much pride and didn't dare give him the satisfaction.

"What the hell, Holly?" he countered, moving as if to step through the doorway. I blocked him, bracing my hands on the sides of the door. "Are you fucking serious?"

"Yes, I'm serious." I felt myself starting to crack inside and clung to my anger, about the only thing keeping me from crying.

Nate had been my friend and my brother's best friend forever. Now, we'd screwed it all up. We'd been intimate, more intimate than I'd been with anyone in my life. No matter what I told myself intellectually, I couldn't forget how I felt when I was with him—all of my hopefulness and wishful thinking spun into the intimacy.

A tiny bit of that vulnerability seeped through. "Look, I can't do this, okay? I told you from the start, I can't do casual. This has to stop. You do what you want with your life, but I can't drag this out. I think you know I want more than you're willing to give."

He stared at me, his eyes narrowing, something flickering in their depths. I was too emotionally strung out to interpret anything with any sense of clarity. I hung onto my control, my hands gripping the edges of the doorframe, as if that would hold me together inside.

"Holly, I told you. That's not all you are to me."

"So you did, but you can't seem to tell me what that means. Just go on your trip." I paused, waiting, perhaps giving him enough time to say something, anything. He said nothing. Steeling myself, I managed to nod. "Good night."

I didn't wait any longer, stepping back quickly and

closing the door. I wasn't usually rude, but I needed to *not* continue this conversation. I slid the bolt shut and ignored it when he called my name and knocked on the door. "This isn't over, Holly."

Wrapping my arms around my waist, I closed my eyes, waiting and listening until I heard his footsteps striking the stairs on the way down. The sound of his truck starting came next. I watched out the windows as he turned out onto Main Street, the glow of his taillights disappearing quickly in the snowy night.

Then, I cried. I had my tea, and I took my bath. None of it made me feel better.

Chapter Twenty-Five

NATE

I leaned back in a chair in front of the fireplace and glanced over at Dave and Nancy. "Don't know how much skiing they'll get in, not in this kind of storm," I observed.

Rolling my head to the side on the back of the chair, I looked out the windows into the darkness. The lights from the lodge illuminated the snow falling. The skies had been clear for my flight up this morning, and then thick clouds rolled in this evening. The snow had started a few hours ago, along with icy winds.

Brenda had made it abundantly clear she would be happy for me to join her tonight. The idea turned my stomach, and it had nothing to do with Brenda. She was still beautiful, flirtatious as ever, and she wanted nothing more than a little fun between the sheets.

A year ago, I'd have happily taken her up on her offer. Tonight, I couldn't even summon the slightest bit of interest. All I could think about was Holly, and how she'd slammed the door in my face the night before.

Brenda, not quite picking up on my cues, sat down in a chair across from me, tucking her feet up under her hips and angling to face me. "So, Nate, how have you been?" she asked, her tone low.

"Oh, busy as ever," I replied.

Dave caught my eye, and I saw the questions swirling in his.

"How many trips do you have booked up here this winter?" he asked. Dave knew me well. While he might not know what the hell was up with me, he seemed to know I preferred to keep this conversation general. "I never know who's handling the flights."

"After this one, I've got two more and then that's it until summer. I could've picked up more, but I prefer to space them out in the winter," I explained.

"I sure wish I could get up here a few more times this winter," Brenda offered with a teasing smile.

This was her cue for me to pick up the other half of the conversation she was trying to start with me. I wasn't quite up for it and was relieved when a few others meandered over to join us. Dave and Nancy kept the conversation moving along, allowing me to mostly stay quiet. A bit later, I stood, giving a wave to the group at large. "Well, I'm gonna pack it in for the night. Here's hoping you guys get some good weather tomorrow morning."

I practically bolted up the stairs, closing and locking my door. That might have seemed a bit ridiculous, but the last time I was here at the same time as Brenda, she had visited me late at night. Tonight, I just wanted to sleep.

The following morning, I was awake before the sun came up. I could still see stars in the sky, wispy gray light creeping in, softening the navy sky to a deep slate blue. After tugging on some clothes, I headed down to the kitchen where I figured I would find Nancy and Dave. Aside from the fact that we were old friends, I came here often enough that they didn't stand on ceremony with me. I had free rein to drop in on their private quarters in the lodge.

I found them just where I expected, with Nancy prepping breakfast and Dave helping as they sipped coffee. Dave glanced up when I came through the door into the kitchen, flashing a grin. "Morning, Nate," he called.

"Coffee's ready," Nancy added by way of greeting, pointing her elbow toward the coffee maker on the counter behind her.

I rounded the large stainless steel table in the center of the kitchen. After helping myself to some coffee, I slipped onto a stool on the opposite side of the table from them. "How's it going this morning?" I asked.

Dave kept chopping potatoes, his knife moving rapidly as he sliced them into thin pieces. "Good, now that I've had almost a full cup of coffee."

"Storm looks like it rolled out overnight. Weather should be better today," I added.

"I'm sure they'll have a good day of skiing. Supposed to be clear tomorrow as well. Are you staying all weekend?" Dave asked.

"I'm not sure. I saw on the flight schedule that Fred Banks will be out here dropping another group on the same day this crew is supposed to fly out. I'm thinking I might ask him to take this peg for me and head back early. If not today, then tomorrow."

Nancy glanced up, her gaze considering." Are you seeing anyone?" she asked.

Dave chuckled as he glanced to her. "Just couldn't help yourself, could you?"

I took a long swallow of my coffee, thinking of Holly the other night and how she shut me out. I wanted the answer to be yes. My hesitation and whatever expression Dave saw on my face must've given something away.

"Well, I'll be damned. You are," he said, his tone wondering.

I took a deep breath, letting it out with a ragged sigh, and ran a hand through my hair. "It's not that simple."

Nancy's eyes widened. "Explain."

"Well, it's Holly."

"Holly Blake?" Dave asked. "Alex's twin sister."

"Yes, that Holly. The thing is, I don't really know what we're doing. The night before I flew out here, she basically told me to fuck off. I think she thought I had some kinda thing going with Brenda."

Dave finished chopping the potatoes and carefully set his knife down. Nancy immediately scooped up the cutting board and poured the potatoes into a large wok on the stove.

"Not that I'm arguing that you have a thing going with Brenda, but I'm pretty sure you had something with her before, right?" Dave asked.

"It was just a weekend," I replied, feeling defensive.

Nancy's gaze shifted to me as she adjusted the heat on the burner, stirring the potatoes and adding some spices. "Right, but Brenda's made her interest in another weekend with you pretty obvious. If Holly saw that, I can see why she might wonder. Have you told her how you feel?"

I must've stared blankly a few beats too long because Dave chuckled. "I'm gonna go with a *no* on that."

I sighed and shrugged. "Well, I mean, I told her she was important to me and..."

Before I even finished a full sentence, Nancy was shaking her head, her gaze stern. When my words trailed off, she gave me a pointed look. "You need to be more clear than that, Nate, if she means something to you. I mean, do you love her? If you do, you need to tell her. You have a reputation for being casual. You're not an ass, but no one expects you to get serious. Anyone who knows you knows that about you. Don't take that as me saying you're a jerk because you're not. You're one of the nicest guys I know. You keep things very low-key when it comes to dating.

"Knowing all that, I'm trying to think of how I perceive you and I'm guessing that's about how Holly perceives you too. I'd figure she thinks that's all this is. To make it even more complicated, her twin brother has been your best friend for years. She's not going to want things to get any messier than they already have. Friend stuff is complicated to begin with."

Nancy rattled all of this off rapidly as she kept adding spices to the potatoes and stirring them in between sips of coffee. At this point, I felt like an idiot. The truth was, I had no idea how to navigate this. I was trying to not push too hard with Holly. Now, I was realizing that might've been a serious miscalculation. Even worse, the fact I was the first man she'd actually had sex with meant everything was all that much more loaded.

I had no idea what Dave and Nancy saw on my face, but they looked at each other and then Nancy asked, "Is there something else?"

"She was a virgin." *Fuck.* That just leapt right out of my mouth. If Holly found out that I shared that detail, she would probably fucking kill me.

I groaned, leaning forward and resting my head in my hands, tunneling my fingers through my hair. When I straightened, two pairs of wide eyes met mine.

"Oh," Nancy said.

"That's it? Oh?" I asked.

Dave snagged his coffee from the counter and took a swift gulp before leveling his gaze with mine again. "Well, that's kind of big. I don't mean to look so surprised."

"Trust me, I was shocked too. It wasn't like she was saving herself or anything. Or at least that's what she said," I muttered.

Nancy had recovered and adjusted the heat on the potatoes, setting a lid over the wok. "Whether she was saving herself or not, that's big."

"I know," I finally said. "She said after the accident..." I glanced at Dave, wondering if he had ever mentioned it to Nancy.

He filled in the blanks for me. Looking to Nancy, he explained, "You know the accident I told you about in high school. It was after I graduated, but a kid died. He was dating Holly."

"Okay," was all Nancy had to offer, although she nodded, indicating she recalled what he meant.

I picked up the thread in the conversation. "Anyway, Holly said everyone just steered clear of her after that. Then, she said it was just one thing after another and before she knew it, she was still a virgin."

"Do you love her?" Nancy asked flatly.

A rush of emotion tightened in my chest. My answer came instantly. I didn't even have to ponder it. "Yes."

"Well, then you better tell her," Nancy said firmly.

"Dude, do whatever Nancy says. I take her advice on all relationship matters," Dave added solemnly.

Nancy burst out laughing and rolled her eyes in his direction. "Not always." Sobering, she glanced back at me. "I just think she needs to know because this will be all kinds of messy if everything is not straight up front. You're an upfront guy. If you love her, then don't let it wait."

"I guess I didn't want to push too hard, too fast. I was afraid she wouldn't trust me," I offered, my own explanation making me wince inside.

"If you don't want your reputation to precede you, you damn well better say something soon," Dave said.

With Nancy and Dave's words echoing in my mind, I borrowed their satellite phone to radio in, and asked Fred to pick up the group when he flew in. Fred affably agreed, but then, he was that kinda guy. I didn't wait and immediately packed up, then said my goodbyes. Although Brenda looked disappointed, she was gracious and headed out for a ski before I left.

As I readied my plane, I calculated I'd be landing in Willow Brook by late afternoon. The skies were clear when I lifted up and stayed that way for a good hour. Then, air traffic control radioed in, telling me to expect some turbulence with a storm passing through. The wind had changed direction, and a storm to the west of us was now blowing east.

Radioing back to air traffic control, I asked for more information. The radio crackled in my ears before the reply came through. "This storm has been blowing out toward the ocean, west of where you are. With the wind shift, it turned back and it's picking up fast. Considering where you need to fly, I'd say you want to get out of the air within the next hour. Find somewhere you can land and wait this out. It shouldn't be long."

"Got it, how far away am I from that summer lodge?"

It wasn't my preference to land and wait this out, but the visibility was getting bad fast. Much as I wanted to get to Holly, even more, I wanted to stay alive.

After reporting in my planned destination, I flew through the thick snow squall that had kicked up, landing safely within the half hour. If the weather had been clear, I'd already have been on the ground in Willow Brook, which made it damn painful to land. I radioed in to confirm my landing, and then trudged through the snow to an empty wilderness lodge. This place didn't have guests in the winter. It was an official emergency shelter for pilots in Alaska, so we could use the gravel runway just above it on a hillside, and had the access code to get into the lodge to wait out any episodes of bad weather.

I would spend the night, warm and dry and with basic food, yet I didn't know whether I'd be able to call Holly. Not that she was expecting to hear from me, but ever since my conversation with Nancy and Dave, I was beyond restless to get to her. I sure as hell didn't appreciate a fucking snowstorm slowing me down.

Chapter Twenty-Six

HOLLY

"Have you heard?" Ella asked.

"Heard what?" I countered, leaning forward to snag a tortilla chip from a bowl in the center of the table.

I'd been looped into regular card nights with Ella. Her sister-in-law, Amelia, and a few other friends hosted these often. They were all friends of mine, although Ella was my closest link. Ever since she'd moved back to Willow Brook, we often came together and hosted gatherings in the rotation.

Tonight, we were at Lucy and Levi's place. Lucy loved card night and had missed a few since she had her baby right after the holidays. Baby Glory was named after Levi's mother, Gloria. At the moment, Lucy held Glory on her lap and was saying something to Amelia. The door to the kitchen opened, and Maisie stepped through, glancing around with a smile.

"Hey everybody," she called as she shrugged out of her jacket, hanging it on the crowded coat rack.

She strode from the kitchen door to the table and

slipped into the only chair left. "Have you heard?" she asked, looking to me.

Chewing my tortilla, I lifted my hands in confusion. "No, but it's weird you just asked me the same thing Ella did," I replied, as I took a sip of water to chase down the tortilla.

"It's Nate. He was on his way back to Willow Brook and had to do an emergency landing during a storm," Maisie explained.

My stomach tightened, anxiety churning in my gut, and worry spinning through me.

"Is he okay?" I blurted out, my voice sounding high and tight.

Maisie nodded, and I fell silent because I didn't know what the hell to say. I had a million questions.

Ella caught my eyes from where she sat across from me. "Caleb heard it from Maisie, and then called up to dispatch in Fairbanks for an update because they're closer," Ella added.

We were sitting at a large round table—me, Ella, Amelia, Lucy, Maisie, and Charlie tonight. Not everyone was here, but close.

"What the hell happened?" I asked, still not able to tamp down my worry. I didn't like the idea of Nate having to make an emergency landing in Alaska in the middle of the wilderness. Not at all.

Maisie took the beer that Amelia handed over when she leaned back to grab it off the kitchen counter. As she took the cap off, she explained, "Exactly that. When he left this morning, the weather was clear where he was and was supposed to be decent. A storm to the west changed direction and went right back into his flight path. Don't worry, he's safe and sound. He already reported back to air traffic control out of Anchorage."

Only now did it occur to me to wonder how anyone other than Ella would think I might be interested to know about this.

"We all know," Lucy said, when she caught me glancing around. She adjusted a sleepy Glory in her arms and flashed a smile.

"Even Glory knows," Amelia said with a slow smile.

My cheeks were flaming. The brief flare of anxiety for Nate had my adrenaline pumping. I looked to Ella.

"I didn't say anything," she protested. "Apparently, Caleb said something to Cade."

"Who said something to Beck," Maisie added with a low laugh. She took a sip of beer and then set the bottle down. "I love my husband, but he's kind of nosy. He's not really a gossip, but he tells me everything. So, he said something to me, and then I asked Amelia, and then... Well, there you have it. Now we all know. What's with the big secret anyway?"

Between my abrupt worry about Nate, not really knowing enough about what happened today, and our one-sided argument the other night, a rush of emotion slammed into me, and I burst into tears.

"Oh God," Lucy said. "Are you okay?"

I grabbed a napkin from the middle of the table and wiped my eyes before taking a shaky breath and nodding. "I'm fine. I think I'm just emotional because you kind of scared me."

"Nate is fine," Maisie said firmly.

"Whatever it is, I'm sure it will be okay," Lucy added. "Or at least that's what I tell myself when I'm up on only two hours of sleep."

Maisie laughed and threw her a sympathetic smile. "I promise, someday Glory will sleep through the night." With two of her own toddlers, Maisie had the most experience with babies at the table.

"Anyway, do tell," Amelia said, circling her hand in the air.

"It's not a big secret," I mumbled.

Charlie cut in. "I think it's the definition of a secret. You had something on the down low with Nate, and none of us knew about it. Except Ella, I guess."

"For what it's worth, I only found out about one night and nothing more," Ella added.

I couldn't help but laugh, even though I was a bit of an emotional wreck. "I haven't talked about it because I didn't want things to get weird. I mean, we're all friends, and Nate is friends with all of you..."

"Yeah, and he's your brother's best friend," Amelia interjected.

"I know. That's *exactly* why I didn't say anything. I don't know what's going on. I mean, we had sex. And—"

"More than once?" Ella cut in.

I bit back a groan. Clearly, Ella felt empowered by the group dynamic here.

"Yes," I said. As I scanned the table, I found curiosity tempered with understanding in the faces looking back at me. They might tease me, but everyone at this table would have my back, and I knew it.

Relaxing, I leaned back in my chair and nodded. "Things have been pretty intense, and I wasn't sure where things were going. Then, well, that woman showed up the other night, and I remembered exactly why I told myself I shouldn't let anything happen between us. For all I know, he's shacked up with her in the middle of a snowstorm now."

Just thinking about that made my heart ache.

"He's alone," Maisie offered.

"How would you even know?" I asked.

"Since I work in dispatch, I can get that kind of information. When I heard that he had to make an emergency landing, I called up to a friend in air traffic control and they told me he was alone in the plane."

I absorbed that bit of information, but it didn't make me feel better.

"So, are you two broken up now?" Lucy asked.

"How can they be broken up when none of us even knew they were together?" Maisie chimed in.

I burst out laughing. With my emotions right at the surface, I couldn't think clearly. "I don't even know if we're together. He tried to come by the other night, and I told him to get lost. Maybe not exactly like that, but that was the point. Now, apparently, he's stranded alone."

"I thought alone was a good thing," Charlie offered.

"It's better than him shacking up with some chick who's got the hots for him, but what if he dies and he's all alone?"

As soon as that question tumbled out, I started crying again. Oh my God. This mess—this tornado of emotion, unreasonable and irrational—was precisely why I should've known better than to let myself get involved with Nate. I didn't know how he felt about me, and I didn't know what to do about any of this.

"Obviously means a lot to you," Ella said, all teasing gone from her tone and her gaze concerned.

I grabbed another napkin and blew my nose as I tried to gather myself together inside. "Yeah, he does, and I don't know what the hell to do about it."

Everyone around the table was quiet. Finally, Amelia spoke. "Maybe you need to talk to him when he gets back, so you can find out where he stands."

"No shit," I retorted, but I was smiling. And crying.

As I blew my nose again, Ham, Levi's cute little brown hamster, came scurrying into the kitchen. He ran over to the window, climbing a series of chairs to get to the windowsill where there was a small bed for him. Yes, Levi had a pet hamster he let run loose in the house.

At the sight of him looking over at us, his whiskers vibrating in the air, I burst out laughing again.

———

Turning over and punching my pillow to adjust it under my

head, I stared out the window, which faced Main Street. Willow Brook turned the streetlights off by nine p.m. That schedule had been determined after a rather testy town hall meeting about light pollution. As minor as the issue seemed, the effect of lights at night was far more evident when you were living on the edge of the wilderness.

Smudgy clouds were hazy in the darkness, with a few stars piercing through the veil. The very clouds were likely the edges of whatever storm had forced Nate to land earlier today. Restless, I grabbed my phone. Maybe, just maybe, he had reception where he was.

Pulling up his number, I tapped the dial button. It rang precisely four times and then the sound of his voicemail picked up.

Hey, it's Nate. In case you missed it, I'm busy. Leave a message and I'll call you back.

This had been his voicemail message for years. Emotion hit me like a wave crashing over, my heart beating hard and fast and my throat thick from tears. God, I missed him. He'd only been gone for a single day and night, and I was a mess.

I didn't leave a message, although I felt quite silly for calling afterwards. I didn't hang up fast enough, so he would have a message of silence from me.

Wiping my nose on the sleeve of my T-shirt, I kicked back the covers to grab some tissues. After a short trek to the bathroom to blow my nose, I returned to my bed, sitting on the edge of the mattress and staring outside. Sleep was hard to come by.

After I finally fell into a restless sleep, my dreams filled with Nate, the vibration of my phone on the nightstand beside my bed woke me in the late morning hours.

In my rush to answer, I almost dropped the phone on the floor. Catching it, I saw Nate's name flashing on the screen for a second. Then, *dropped call.*

When I frantically called him back, I didn't even get to his voicemail before the call dropped.

Chapter Twenty-Seven

NATE

Holly's phone rang in my ear, and I waited, praying she would answer. I wasn't much of a praying man. Resorting to prayer said something about how desperately I wanted to hear her voice.

Nancy's pointed words about making sure to let Holly know how I felt in the context of my reputation preceding me had been beating like a drum in my brain all night. Unlike Nancy and Dave's lodge, the lodge where I had landed wasn't tricked out for winter. Aside from a back-up propane generator, which kept the temperature above freezing and the power running for refrigeration food storage, the satellite cable was turned off, and there was no cell phone reception. On the ground, in the middle of nowhere, I sure as hell hadn't been able to call anyone. I had asked air traffic control to notify Willow Brook dispatch of my status when I landed. Considering that I'd been expected to arrive there yesterday afternoon, I didn't want anybody worrying.

On the third ring, Holly's voicemail picked up. "Fuck," I muttered to myself as I listened to her voice.

Hey, hey, you know who it is if you're calling. Leave a message,
and I'll call you back when I can.

A smile tugged at the corners of my mouth at the sound
of her voice. I was damn tempted to tell her how I felt via
voicemail, yet somehow that didn't seem quite right.

"Hey, Holly, it's Nate. I saw that I had a missed call from
you. I'm sure you figured out I didn't have any reception last
night. I tried earlier this morning, but the reception was still
shit. I'm in the air now, and I should be in Willow Brook
within the hour."

Hanging up, I tossed my phone into the cup holder in
between the seats and then radioed in to confirm my estimated time of arrival. I'd waited for the clouds to dissipate
before leaving. The sky was clear early this afternoon, a
bright blue canvas with the sun rising above the mountains.
The wind was behind me, helping to make up a little time on
the way. With thoughts of Holly spinning through my mind,
there was only one thing I wanted to know—whether she
felt even remotely close to the way I did.

My flight path brought me into Willow Brook from the
east. As fucking bad luck would have it, a pair of seagulls
flew directly in front of the plane, getting sucked into one of
my engines.

"For fuck's sake," I muttered as I radioed in to report it,
wrestling to manage the plane with one engine knocked out.

Chapter Twenty-Eight

HOLLY

Maisie looked up from behind the counter in the dispatch area at Willow Brook Fire & Rescue. She shook her head, her brown curls bouncing. "If Nate left you a message, obviously he's fine. If I had anything to tell you, I promise I would."

Biting my lip, I looked away, mentally trying to calm down. I'd been edgy and restless all morning. I was running on maybe an hour or so of sleep as it was. Then, I realized Nate had actually called me back while I was in the shower, and I'd missed his call. That had only amped up the tension thrumming inside of me.

Too frustrated to even consider going in to work, I called out for my afternoon shift, which I almost never did. Chris had offered to cover for me and gave me a little pep talk. He told me it was obvious I was in love with Nate and to do something about it instead of dallying around it.

Now, I was here because I figured Maisie could give me answers, specifically Nate's estimated time of arrival. Maisie took a phone call while I pushed away from the counter surrounding her and paced in front of the windows with my arms tightly crossed.

I heard her saying goodbye to whomever was on the call. After a few beats of quiet, she caught my eye on one of my pacing cycles. "You know, I think maybe you need to take a nice long look at how you're feeling," she called over.

Turning in my loop, I detoured back to where she sat at her desk. "Look at what?"

She rolled her eyes and shook her head slowly. Maisie took adorable to new levels with her curly brown hair, round cheeks, wide brown eyes, and freckles. She was funny and blunt, which I usually appreciated. She and I had that in common. Right now, I was wishing she would be a bit more clear.

"What do you mean?"

"You're in love with Nate and now you need to deal with it," she replied promptly, making me curse her bluntness.

"You don't know that," I retorted, defensiveness rising inside.

Undeterred, Maisie rolled her eyes again. "Yes, I do. I know it when I see it. It's like porn."

"Love is like porn?"

"Oh my God." She took her headphones off and buried her face in her hands. When she looked up, she shook her head again.

"I didn't mean love was like porn. Remember that whole Supreme Court case where the justice said, 'I know it when I see it'?"

"Um, I think so," I replied, my memory nudged enough that I had a vague idea what she meant.

"One of the justices was referring to how he knew when something met the threshold for obscenity," Maisie explained. When I cocked my head in question, because honestly, I didn't know how she had this buried in her memory bank, she added, "I once thought I wanted to go to law school but then I changed my mind. Anyway, we're off on a tangent, and it's totally my fault. I'm just saying it's pretty obvious to me you love Nate."

My heart was beating so hard, it actually hurt. I figured, at this rate, I would have bruises inside my chest. My stomach was spinning in flips, a mixture of anxiety, worry, and fear.

The moment Maisie said the word *love* out loud, my pulse had taken off at a gallop. I hadn't even allowed that word to pass through my mind when it came to Nate. It was a forbidden word. I wasn't permitted to let myself think that.

It was complicated enough that I was having sex with him, that I lost my virginity to him, and that I couldn't stop thinking about him. The other night, when I saw that woman trying to flirt with him, illuminated the entire mess. Just thinking about it sent another hot flash of anger and embarrassment through me. I didn't like to think of myself as the kind of woman who got jealous. I liked to think I knew better when it came to getting involved with a man who'd done nothing to show he was interested in anything serious. But my body and my heart didn't seem to be listening to my intellect.

"You think so? Really?" I asked, almost desperate for Maisie to reconsider.

Maisie nodded slowly, her eyes softening as she looked at me. "This part sucks. It totally sucks."

"How would you know? Beck is so in love with you, it's almost ridiculous. You two are still all gaga for each other, and that's with two kids."

Maisie burst out laughing. "We fight. Plenty. Trust me. I don't think you really knew me when I first moved here, but I was kind of bitchy. I didn't exactly fall in Beck's arms."

A disbelieving laugh escaped. "Really?"

I could kind of see it now that she mentioned it. Maisie had a sharp edge to her, and she was blunt and sarcastic. I knew her childhood hadn't been all that great. Yet, I hadn't gotten to know her until after she and Beck were already together. I'd gotten closer to her after Ella moved back to Willow Brook and started having me tag along to card nights.

Taking a deep breath and willing my heart to stop pounding so hard, I eyed her. "What should I do?" I asked. I loved answers. That's why I'd been such a good student. I graduated at the top of my high school class, my college class, and my nursing school class. I loved knowing the answers because it made me feel like life made sense. I didn't appreciate the mess of emotions and uncertainty I was currently experiencing. Not one bit.

My heart was acting crazy, and I couldn't stop thinking about Nate last night. I hardly slept at all because I'd been worried about him. Even though the idea of him being shacked up in a snowstorm at an empty wilderness lodge with a woman made my stomach turn, I didn't like the idea of him being alone either.

"The obvious answer is you need to talk to him," Maisie said, her tone gentle.

Emotion twisted inside again, my heart thumping erratically. Just the idea of trying to be open about my feelings terrified me. If Nate never knew how I felt, then I wouldn't have to experience rejection. We could somehow patch up our friendship, and I'd learn how to move on.

When I didn't respond, Maisie picked up the thread. "No matter what's going to happen between you two, it's already messy. You can't go back to just being friends. The way I see it, you need to just push through this. It's like walking through fire."

"Walking through fire?" I felt like I was on repeat with everything she said.

Maisie cocked her head to the side. "Not literally, but maybe emotionally. Just tell him how you feel and figure it out from there."

My heart kept up its wild beat. At that moment, the station phone rang. She snagged her headset and quickly answered.

"Oh. Is he okay?" She was quiet for a moment, listening to whatever was being said on the other end of the call. I had no idea who she was talking about. Her eyes flicked up to me, concern contained there.

"What?" I demanded.

Maisie held a finger up, jotting something down on a notepad before she ended the call. Looking up to me, her gaze was carefully unreadable. "Nate's fine. He's out at the small airport on the far side of town. A pair of seagulls got sucked into one of the engines, so it made for a rough landing. He's fine, totally fine. That was Rex, calling to let me know they were just calling it in now because he was down the road and saw it."

I didn't even bother to reply. The word *fine* was ringing through my head as I ran out the door and jumped in my car.

But I didn't miss the hint of a smile on Maisie's face as I left.

Chapter Twenty-Nine

HOLLY

Willow Brook's airport, if you could call it that, was on the outskirts of town past the hospital. There were a few plane hangars there and a small runway with nothing more. I'd been here before with Alex, although I never thought much about the fact it was definitely Nate's territory. He owned two of the hangars here.

The road shifted from pavement to gravel when I turned off on the side road that led down to the airport. Although the road was plowed, as I came around the corner, my car skidded slightly on the slick surface. My heartbeat, already racing, sped slightly. I eased off the gas and turned into the slide. Fortunately, I'd been driving on winter roads ever since I'd known how to drive. With little trouble, I was able to get my car back under control.

When the runway came into view, I saw the whopping total of two police cars from Willow Brook there, along with an emergency vehicle. Only then did I recall Maisie had mentioned Rex had been close enough to see Nate's landing. I hadn't given her a chance to say anything else.

Slamming my car door, I hurried across the parking lot out toward the runway, my eyes scanning for Nate. Although Maisie had clearly told me he was perfectly fine, it didn't ease my worry. The plane sat at an angle on the runway, slightly tilted. It looked as if one of its wheels had been damaged in the landing.

My eyes finally caught sight of Nate with his hand resting on the nose of the plane, talking to Rex Masters, Willow Brook's police chief and Ella's father. I didn't even absorb who else was present, breaking into a run the moment I saw Nate.

With my heart in my throat, I was running and then I was falling, my foot catching on a rock. The snow flanking the runway was slick enough that it was almost like ice. Runways in rural Alaska weren't quite what most people considered when they thought of runways. They were rarely paved, and while they might be maintained, landing on gravel and packed snow was a necessary part of life for wilderness pilots. Willow Brook kept the runway salted and sanded, but everything around it was left alone.

I crashed against the frozen ground with a grunt. Pain shot from my hip and radiated through my legs. Frozen ground was completely unforgiving. There wasn't even a little bit of cushion to it.

I lost my breath and tears pricked at my eyes for a moment. The pain was sharp. Ignoring it, I started to scramble up. Of course, my clumsy approach had drawn every eye toward me. When I looked up, I saw Nate jogging over, slowing as he crossed over from the sanded and salted runway onto the icy ground.

"Hey, are you okay?" he called.

Seeing as I still hadn't caught my breath, he was at my side before I could answer. Kneeling down, his dark chocolate gaze coasted over me. The moment his eyes met mine, all the emotions I'd been holding at bay for what felt like weeks now burst forth, like a wave crashing onto the sand. Tears rolled down my cheeks as I nodded.

The concern in his gaze deepened. "Are you sure?"

I nodded again, and he started to pull me into his arms when another pair of boots came into my line of sight.

Glancing up, I saw Rex had followed Nate over, along with Caleb. Seeing as Rex was practically a father to me, with Ella as my best friend growing up, I couldn't just ignore him. Of course, Caleb would want to see what was going on too. I didn't quite want to deal with a crowd though. I felt raw, exposed, and vulnerable. I was also cold and the pain was setting in my hip. While the sharpness faded, a dull, throbbing ache settled there.

"You sure you're okay?" Rex asked.

Nate glanced up. "We need a minute," he said quickly.

Caleb caught my eyes. Quick to read the room, so to speak, he simply nodded and turned away, nudging Rex when he started to ask another question. Rex's piercing gaze bounced between Nate and me before awareness appeared to click into place. He nodded and turned with Caleb. They walked back toward the plane together.

When they were out of earshot again, Nate's hand slid down my arm, resting at the crook of my elbow. I was sitting in a not-so-elegant position on the packed snow, with one knee bent awkwardly and my other leg splayed on the ground. "I'm fine," I murmured as a tear escaped.

"Okay. I called you earlier, did you get my message?" he asked.

Staring into his eyes, I felt another tear roll down my cheek, cool against my skin. Emotion was rushing through me. Falling on my ass about summed up how I felt inside. I hadn't thought through any of this. Pure emotion had driven me here, and now Nate was here, perfectly fine. Just as Maisie told me.

Although we didn't say a word, it felt as if we communicated somehow. For a long moment, we just looked at each other, and then Nate leaned forward, pressing his lips to my cheek and dusting a few kisses on the way to my mouth. He lingered there briefly, the point of contact a searing heat in contrast to the cold surrounding us.

The moment was brief, but so intense my heart was pounding wildly in my chest by the time he drew away.

"I think we probably need to talk," he said, his voice gruff. "But..."

"I think I love you," I blurted out. The words simply flew out of my mouth.

He stared at me, just long enough to make me wish I could snatch those words back. Me and my big mouth. This most definitely wasn't the first time my words had gotten ahead of my brain.

His eyes blazed fiercely. "Well, that's good. Because I don't think I love you. I *know* I do."

That sent me into a bout of full-on crying.

At that point, Dana, one of the EMTs, came jogging over, likely thinking I injured myself in the fall and my crying had something to do with it. "Are you okay?" she called as she hurried over.

I gulped in a few shaky breaths and sniffled, dragging the sleeve of my jacket across my nose.

"We're kind of stuck with the audience. I've got to take care of some official things because one of my engines got knocked out. Unfortunately, I can't just walk away right now," Nate said, his voice low.

"I know." I started to clamber to my feet only to slip again in the process. "Ouch," I muttered, landing on the same hip. My poor hip. Catching Nate's gaze, I shook my head. "I might have a fat ass, but landing on the side hurts."

"I happen to love that ass," he replied with a grin just as Dana reached us.

"I'm fine, I swear," I said, glancing up into her concerned gaze. It was a relief, in a way, to have this fuss around me. I was spinning on the currents of my emotions, overwhelmed and raw inside. It helped to have something other than Nate to focus on.

Dana glanced between Nate and me. If she picked up on anything, she didn't say so. "You sure?" she asked as Nate helped me up.

"I am. I'm sure I'm gonna have a nasty bruise on my hip, but otherwise, I'm fine."

I stepped gingerly, feeling the pain shoot out from my hip. I was a bit gimpy, but I walked alongside them toward Nate's plane.

"You gonna hang around?" Nate asked as Dana veered off towards the emergency vehicle.

"Uh huh. I don't even see your truck here," I said, looking around.

"Caleb dropped me off yesterday. I scheduled an oil change while I was gone, so he's here to pick me up. I'm guessing I can ride with you, though," he said, barely a hint of a question in his tone.

"Of course."

"You sure?"

"I'm not going anywhere," I said firmly, feeling my usual spark return in the midst of the emotional storm.

He chuckled, sliding his hand down my back as Rex approached us again. "Why is the ambulance here?" I asked.

"Because they were right down the road at the hospital when I got the call from air traffic control. We knew he was fine. But it was a two-minute drive, so they came, just in case," Rex explained. He looked to Nate. "Let's do the official paperwork."

Rex and Nate conferred while Rex entered everything into a computer tablet and took a few photos of the plane. While I waited on the back bumper of the ambulance, shivering slightly from the cold, Caleb walked over and stopped in front of me.

"I hear my taxi services aren't needed," he said with a grin.

I couldn't help but smile in return. "I'll take Nate home."

Caleb looked at me for a long moment, his gaze sobering. "About damn time."

"Huh?"

"You and Nate."

Chapter Thirty

NATE

By the time I wrapped everything up with the plane, it was getting late. Rex hurried things along, but it had been mid-afternoon when I landed as it was. The ambulance was gone, my brother had left, and it was just Rex, Holly, and me as the sun was dipping down the horizon. Holly had stubbornly insisted on waiting outside, but I could tell she was cold when Rex and I finally finished.

She was shivering in her bright blue down jacket. She stood there in her jeans and boots, her eyes on me as I walked over.

"I could've taken him home, you know," Rex offered with a sly grin.

Holly was unperturbed and simply narrowed her eyes. "Not necessary. That's why I'm here."

Rex chuckled, slapping me on the shoulder as he walked by to climb into his patrol car. Then, it was just Holly and me standing alone, the sound of Rex's car fading in the distance as he drove away.

My plane was in the hangar, and Holly's car waited in the parking area on the far side of the runway. I stopped in front of her, sliding my hands into her pockets where she had hers tucked. "You're cold," I said as I stepped closer to her.

Her hands were chilly as I curled mine over hers. I'd never thought much about pockets, but just now, I was thinking it was damn awesome that her jacket had large pockets, roomy enough for my hands to fit around hers.

"A little," she replied. "You ready?"

"Absolutely."

I couldn't help it, I had to kiss her. Her cheeks were flushed and her eyes were bright in the gloaming. The smattering of freckles across her nose and cheeks stood out. Bending low, I brought my lips to hers, just brushing across them. Her lips were warm, and a *zing* of electricity passed between us. I smiled against her mouth because I couldn't help it. I was so damn relieved and so damn happy. I felt her smile in response.

"What?" she murmured, the motion of her lips against mine like flint striking against my desire. Holly was too much. All she had to do was be near me and lust owned my body.

"Just glad you're here." I swept my tongue across the seam of her lips, a low groan escaping.

The warm sweetness of her mouth invited me in. As was always the case, the moment I kissed Holly, it got hot. Fast. Her tongue slid sensually against mine and she stepped closer. Freeing one of her hands from her pockets, she pulled me hard against her, letting out another gasp when I tore my lips free, blazing a trail down her neck, needing to taste the salty sweetness of her skin.

A gust of wind blew, cold and harsh, and her skin pebbled under my lips. Lifting my head, I looked at her and my cock swelled. Her lips were pink and swollen from our kiss and her breath came in little pants, misting the air between us.

"Let's go," I said, my voice rough with emotion and desire.

Curling one of my hands around hers, I turned, not

wanting to move away from her, not at all, but we needed to get somewhere warm. We walked across the runway toward her car, the sky above us stained pink with darkness coming to claim the day. The mountains in the distance were dark outlines, with a few stars glittering in the early evening. Another gust of winter wind blew across the runway, sending the ends of Holly's hair into a swirl, the blonde bright in the fading light.

———

Holly declared that we were going to my place as soon as we got in her car. "But your place is closer," I pointed out.

I wasn't ashamed to admit I was feeling greedy. I wanted her bare naked with me buried inside of her as soon as feasibly possible. She reached forward to adjust the heat, glancing over at me. "But your bed is better."

I laughed, a sense of unfamiliar joy clenching my heart like a fist. There were many things I had never expected to happen. Actually, getting a shot with Holly was definitely one of them. Life had gotten in the way and taken us each on our own detours.

"My place it is, then."

A brief drive later, we were stomping snow off our boots and walking into my house. The drive over had been a form of sweet torture. The roads were slick so I had kept my hands to myself. Holly had taken it upon herself to tease me. Despite my protests, she had my cock rock hard and my jeans unbuttoned on the ride over, completely ignoring my point that the roads were slick.

I got my revenge. The moment the door was closed behind us, I spun her around and caught her laugh in a kiss.

Everything happened fast. Our clothes were left in a tangle on the floor, marking our path across my living room and up the stairs. Her panties were the last to go, falling over the railing outside my bedroom door and landing on the kitchen island below.

Holly was panting, gasping, and dripping wet when I sank my fingers inside of her. She stumbled and caught her balance on the railing. I'd given her no mercy, already sending her flying once with my fingers and tongue at the bottom of the stairs. I was close to losing control with pre-cum dripping down along my cock.

When I looked down, I couldn't resist sliding a hand over the curve of her lush bottom, curling my fist around my cock with the other. She got right with the program, bending over the railing as I dragged the head of my cock through her folds. Her juices coated me.

"Jesus, Holly," I murmured. "I fucking missed you."

Her answer was a low groan as I slid through her folds again before sinking deeply inside of her, slowly, oh-so-slowly, and I could feel every slick inch of her channel pulsing around me. She gasped when I slid back inside again as her hips pushed back into my thrust .

"That was too fucking long to be away from you," I murmured.

She cried out when I filled her again. I needed more, I needed to see her. Drawing back quickly, I spun her around and lifted her in my arms, shouldering through my bedroom door. As soon as we reached my bed, I stretched out over her, sinking inside of her. Her hips rose to meet me, her legs gripping me, and her skin silky against mine.

I held still, rising up on an elbow and brushing her hair away from her face. "I need to know something," I murmured, my voice gruff with emotion. My heart squeezed again, thudding hard and fast in my chest. Her eyes opened, colliding with mine. "When did you know you loved me?"

She stared at me for a moment, her breasts pressing against my chest with every ragged breath. Vulnerability flashed in her eyes. I continued, "Because I knew a long time ago. Maybe not exactly, but it was there. All the way back in high school."

Her eyes widened and her breath hitched. "Oh," she said, a tear suddenly rolling down her cheek. "I didn't know very much back then, but I wanted you and then everything got a little crazy," she said softly.

"I know."

"To answer your question, I think I probably knew last year. It scared me."

My throat was tight with emotion, but it was okay. Because this was Holly, this was me, and this was exactly how it was supposed to be.

"I knew then, and I wasn't ready to face it. You were my fantasy for too long."

Her eyes widened again. "Your fantasy?"

I nodded slowly. "For years."

At that, I caught her lips in a kiss and finally, *finally*, drew back and sank inside of her again. I knew she was close, because I knew her body. After a few strokes, I reached between us, swirling my thumb over her swollen clit as I buried myself inside of her tight, slick heat.

She cried out sharply, her head falling back into the pillows as her body trembled and her channel clamped down around me. I finally let go, my climax slamming through me as I spent myself inside of her. Collapsing against her, I eased my weight to the side. But I didn't want to move, didn't want to sever our joining.

As we lay there, catching our breath, Holly laughed softly.

"What's so funny?"

"Tomorrow is Valentine's Day. I guess I'll finally get to make good on that date you bought."

I burst out laughing. "Damn straight. You owe me."

EPILOGUE

Holly

Once again, I found myself backstage at a fundraiser in Anchorage. Once again, I was also stuffed into a skimpy nurse's outfit. There were two major differences tonight. One: it wasn't Halloween. Instead, it was Valentine's Day. Two: I was only wearing this nurse's costume after Nate begged me to.

I smiled to myself as I adjusted the top and then rolled my eyes. Yet again, my rather generous boobs were threatening to spill out the top. I told Nate he'd only get to see me in this outfit for a few minutes and that was it.

When Megan had asked me to do another fundraiser this year, I refused to do the Halloween one. She conveniently left out the fact that the dressing up part had nothing to do with Halloween. They auctioned off dates at all of them and made a ton of money.

Nate and I had had a bit of an argument over the fact he was already planning to spend five thousand dollars—or more, if necessary—to win the date with me. He insisted it was for a good cause. One thing I had learned in the year since last Valentine's Day was there were many things I hadn't known about Nate.

Despite the fact that I assumed I had known him well because we'd grown up together, there was a lot I didn't. For example, I hadn't realized how financially comfortable he was. Oh, it was nothing ridiculous, like being a billionaire. But he made damn good money as a pilot, and he was smart with investing it wisely and continuing to build his business. Just a few months ago, he rolled a bundle of money into a new wilderness lodge that was being built roughly an hour north of Willow Brook. My point was, he wasn't worried about spending another five grand. When I pointed out that he could just make a direct donation to the hospital fund, he told me there was no way in hell he was letting someone else win a date with me.

Recalling that argument and the crazy, hot make-up sex that followed it, I flushed as I spun away from the mirror. Strolling out of the dressing room, I realized this was the first time since Halloween a year and a half ago now that I'd worn heels. That just went to show how little I bothered with my appearance most days. I paused beside the makeshift bar set up backstage. Ethan was there, dapper in a pinstriped gray suit. Tonight, another man was manning the bar with him, no pun intended.

"Well, hello, Holly," Ethan said with a smile. "I don't think you met my husband, Jack, last year. Jack"—he gestured between us—"this is Holly. Last year, she set a record donation for her date. We're hoping she makes us just as much money this year." He looked at me and winked. "How many shots of tequila this time?"

"Just one," I replied with a grin. "I need something to keep my nerve. As far as that donation, I have a guarantee."

"A guarantee?" Jack asked. They made a handsome pair. Ethan, with his black hair flecked with silver, and blue eyes, and Jack, with his steel silver hair and even brighter blue eyes. Both he and Ethan had a teasing glint in their gazes, the easy affection between them clear.

"Yes. Remember my date last year?" I asked, looking to Ethan.

"Oh yes. You were quite flustered with the whole situation afterwards. Although..." He paused, his eyes narrowing.

"What?"

"Oh no, you finish."

"I was just going to say it was obvious to me that you liked your date, even if you were cranky about him winning," Ethan added with a slow smile.

"I did like him. In fact, he's my husband now."

Ethan clapped his hands and rounded the table to pull me into a quick hug. "This is perfect! We have to use it in our advertising materials for the next one. One of our dates led to a happily-ever-after." Ethan glanced to Jack, who simply chuckled and shrugged.

"Unless you tell him no, you'll be all over those ads," Jack warned.

I shrugged. "That's fine. If it raises more money, I'm all for it."

Jack poured me a generous shot of tequila, and we chatted while I waited for Megan to fetch me to go out on stage.

Once again, the glare from the lights kept me from being able to see much beyond the front row, but when I heard Nate's voice calling out, a little thrill ran through me. When my turn was over, I strolled back across the stage, giving Megan a high-five as I passed by, and a thumbs-up to the next guy headed out on the stage, looking none-too-thrilled.

Ethan escorted me back to the room to wait for my "date." Unlike last time, I wasn't nervous and worried about who had purchased a few hours of my time.

Moments later, the door opened and I turned to look at Nate. He shut the door behind him and held still. I was quite convinced I'd never get tired of looking at him. His brown hair was shaggy, and his eyes dark. Even though all he wore was jeans and a T-shirt, his muscled frame was easily visible.

"Get over here," I ordered, my pulse thumping with the heat banked in his gaze flaring to life. He closed the short distance between us.

"This time, you better not make me wait for my date. I want it tonight," he said when he got right in front of me.

He stepped closer, sliding a hand down my spine, not even bothering to waste time. He flipped my skirt up, his warm palm cupping my bottom.

"Holly, you're not wearing any underwear," he murmured gruffly. His fingers teased along the curve of my ass, sliding into the cleft between my thighs.

"Uh-uh," I gasped.

A hot shiver raced through me when he dipped his head, laving his tongue over the sensitive skin right behind my ear. Goose bumps prickled over the surface of my skin. When he lifted his head, his eyes darkened further. The look contained there was so intense, he took my breath away. My heart was pounding, and my belly clenching.

He trailed his fingers through the slick, wet heat of my pussy. I had meant to tease him. Yet, I constantly forgot that he drove me insane. Right now, what I needed was him inside of me and nothing else.

"I need you," I whispered urgently.

Another thing I had learned about Nate was he made sure I got what I needed, when I needed it. Although I had no one for comparison for the full act, so to speak, I'd had plenty of experience with foreplay. No one even came close to the way Nate made me feel. In a flash, he spun us around, locking the door as he backed me against it. With a bit of fumbling, we freed his cock, and he buried himself inside me. It was hot, fast, and rushed.

Afterwards, he waited while I discarded my silly nurse costume and changed into jeans and a sweater. He caught my hand in his as we walked out. Ethan and Jack were still at the bar because the night was nowhere near over. "Where to, lovebirds?" Jack asked with a wink.

I looked up to Nate. "Where did you want to have dinner?" I asked.

"You promised me a burger."

With a laugh, I walked outside with him right beside me every step of the way. It was freezing, of course. It was February in Alaska, the deepest part of winter.

"We never did make it here for a date last year," Nate said, his eyes cutting sideways to catch mine.

"No, we didn't. I guess I owe you two dates."

A giddy sense of joy bubbled up inside me. There was fantasy, and then there was reality. When it came to Nate and me, reality was so much better.

————

NATE

I was standing downstairs in the kitchen, waiting for the coffee to finish and for Holly to come downstairs. Striding over to the windows, I looked outside. The landscape was covered in dazzling frost. Everything glittered under the sun's rays. I heard footsteps and turned to look upstairs. Holly's blonde hair was dark since it was damp from her shower, and she wore sweatpants, bulky wool socks, and a T-shirt. Objectively speaking, what she was wearing wasn't sexy. But to me, Holly could literally wear a paper bag, and she'd take my breath away. As she came down the stairs, I noticed that her cheeks were flushed.

"What?" I asked.

"Nothing."

"Nothing?"

She giggled. "Okay, maybe not nothing."

I pulled her close. I loved that life with Holly was like

unwrapping a present, day by day. I thought I'd known everything about her. I hadn't. The big secret of her virginity still shocked me a bit. Since last year, I'd discovered her stubbornness ran deeper than I thought. I didn't care. Not even a little.

She had a soft side I hadn't seen much before. She was so brash and sassy. That was the part of her I'd known so well. It was definitely one side of her, but only one. She loved the animal shelter and visited often. We had since adopted two mutts. Our best guesses were that one of them was a husky mix and the other, a lab mix.

"I might be late," she finally said, tipping her head back to look at me.

My heart gave a quick tumble. "What? Are you sure?"

"I'm sure I'm late, but I'm not sure what that means. So, I can't have coffee," she said suddenly.

"Coffee?"

She shook her head. "My body is a vessel now, and I have to treat it perfectly."

Something else I had learned about Holly was she desperately wanted kids. I was *all* about that. Especially because it meant we got to have lots of sex. Although, with the way we were, that was a foregone conclusion.

Many hours later, after a test confirmed that Holly was pregnant, she was snuggled up against my side on the couch with the television droning in the back around.

My favorite thing about being with Holly? These moments. The mundane ones. The ones where it was just *us* existing in space and time together.

I rolled my head to the side, breathing in the scent of her hair. "Have I mentioned that I am so fucking relieved we figured this out?"

"Figured what out?" she asked, her eyes glinting with a smile when she looked up at me.

"That you were meant to be mine," I murmured, catching her lips in a kiss.

Because it was Holly, and she *had* to have the last word, she drew back with a giggle. "Oh no, you were meant to be *mine*."

———

Thank you for reading Burn For You - I hope you loved Holly & Nate's story!

Up next in the Into the Fire Series is Crash & Burn - Remy & Rachel's story.

Remy is the strong, silent type—the kind of man who makes you swoon on sight. Rachel is sexy & sassy , but her life went on the skids after a disastrous relationship. Remy just might be about to sweep her off her feet. Don't miss their story!

Keep reading for a sneak peek!

Be sure to sign up for my newsletter for the latest news, teasers & more! Click here to sign up: http://jhcroixauthor.com/subscribe/

EXCERPT: CRASH & BURN

Rachel

"Henry!"

My dog, the aforementioned Henry, had just bolted away from me. I picked up my jog to a flat out run, mud splashing on my face as one of my feet slammed into a puddle.

"Dammit, Henry," I muttered to myself.

Ahead of me on the trail, he looked back, covered in mud with his long tail wagging back and forth. I couldn't help but laugh. I loved my dog, but he was nuts. Black and gold with silky fur, he was full of energy and adventure.

We were taking one of our usual runs. Now that it was the early spring, or rather mud season, as it was best known in Alaska, it was warm enough to get outside more often. For a moment, I thought Henry was done with his fun, but he looked away and kept on running, appearing to think this was a game.

"Henry!"

At this rate, he would probably make it all the way back to the car before I caught up to him.

That's fine. I need more exercise anyway. My ass is big enough already.

Coming around the corner on the trail, I let out a yelp when I almost collided with someone. My feet skidded in the mud, and I fell into an inglorious heap.

"Ouch!" I exclaimed as my knee collided with a rock somewhere in the mud.

Rising up slightly on my hands, I glanced down at my muddy legs and shirt. I'd fallen in the edge of a puddle and was now soaked and covered in muck. When I looked up, my gaze ran smack into Remy Martin. "Oh shit."

Of course I said that out loud.

You see, Remy was sexy as hell. At the moment, he happened to be wearing a pair of running shorts that molded to his legs, which were nothing but muscle. *He* was nothing but muscle.

My eyes traveled up his legs across his muscled chest. His heather gray T-shirt was damp with sweat and conveniently —as far as my eyes were concerned, that is—delineated every muscle of said sexy chest. When my gaze traveled to his face, mossy green eyes met mine, his dark blond hair mussed. Although his skin had a light sheen of sweat, he appeared barely winded.

"Oh shit?" he asked after staring at me for a moment. "Are you mad at me for existing?" His slow southern drawl slid over me. Remy's voice was like honey and whiskey—rich with a hint of sweet, and so damn sexy. Just hearing him speak sent heat spinning through me.

Fuck. This time, I kept my profanity to myself. I was sitting here, covered in mud, with the hottest man in town staring down at me. I felt my cheeks heating and was relieved I had mud on my face because perhaps it would obscure my blush.

"I was mad at the puddle, not you," I replied, only half-lying. I *was* mad at the puddle, but I was also horrified to be in this state in his presence.

With a shake of my head, I moved to scramble to my

feet. I managed to get halfway up and then my foot slid out from under me again. Because it was *that* kind of day.

Remy held a hand out, and I bit my lip with a sigh. Reaching up, his strong grip curled around my hand as he pulled me up easily. Once I was upright, he stepped back, making sure I was fully out of the puddle and on firmer ground before he released me.

His eyes coasted over me. "Are you okay?"

Embarrassed, flustered, and annoyed as hell at my body's swift reaction to Remy's presence, I managed to nod. "I'm fine, just a little dirty. Thanks for helping me up," I said with a wry smile, gesturing at the mud streaks on my legs.

Remy's mouth kicked up at one corner in a half-grin. Sweet hell, his grins should be illegal. My lower belly clenched and heat radiated outward.

"Anytime, darlin'," he replied, his grin stretching to the other side of his mouth. "I presume that was your dog who just ran past me?" One of his brows hitched up.

I had completely forgotten about Henry. That just went to show how easily Remy rattled me. "Yes, oh God, I need to catch up to him."

As I started to turn, Remy put his hand on my elbow. Before I could say a word, he spoke. "Wait."

The word was low, and somehow authoritative. But then, everything about Remy was powerful and authoritative. Oh, and sexy as hell. Did I mention that yet?

The man practically dripped sex with his southern drawl, his fit, muscled body, and his dangerously heated gaze. To top it all off—nature really had been too generous with him —he had chiseled features, high cheekbones, and full lips. The man could've been a model. Yet, he seemed oblivious to his effect on women. He was always gracious and polite.

I had two conflicting impulses whenever I was near Remy. I wanted to throw myself at him. And, I wanted to curl up in his arms and be held, to have his strength wrapped around me. Remy was that kind of man, the kind you knew would save you if you needed saving.

Before I even had a chance to ask why Remy wanted me to wait, Henry appeared, dashing toward us and stopping right in front of Remy. Looking down at him, I couldn't help but laugh. "*Of course* you come when I'm not even calling."

Henry wagged his entire body, practically vibrating when Remy dropped his hand from my elbow and knelt down to pet him. Remy didn't seem to care one bit that Henry was covered head to toe in mud and was licking his face all over. Even my dog liked Remy.

When Remy straightened, Henry circled around my legs, and I reached down to pet him. It didn't matter if he got mud on me because I was already covered in it. I looked over at Remy. "Thanks again for helping me up."

Remy smiled, his gorgeous green eyes crinkling at the corners. "Anytime, darlin'." He was quiet for a beat, his gaze considering. "You sure you're okay?"

"I'm fine. Just in serious need of a shower." Leaning down, I clipped Henry's leash on his collar. He didn't usually dash off, but I preferred to keep him close until we were back in my car. "Thanks again," I said with a wave as I started to walk. When I took a step, sharp pain shot from my knee. A gasp hissed through my teeth when I paused.

Remy was back at my side in a flash. "I'll walk you back."

"Oh my God, I can walk, Remy. I banged my knee when I fell. It's no biggie," I insisted.

He ignored me and stepped to the side where Henry was, taking the leash from me and sliding his other hand into the crook of my elbow. "I can't let you walk back alone. The last thing I want is for you to slip and fall again."

I wanted to argue, but I sensed Remy was going to walk with me, whether I argued the point or not. "Fine," I muttered.

We didn't have far to go. Within a few minutes, we

reached the parking lot at the base of the trail. I let Henry into the back of my car, and he immediately started lapping up water from his travel bowl.

Remy grinned. "Smart," he said, gesturing to the towels layered on the carpet in the back of my small SUV.

"Oh, I'm always prepared for Henry to get dirty." I closed the back of the SUV when Henry curled up and rested his chin on his paws, checking to make sure the windows in the back were cracked open.

Turning to look at Remy, I caught him taking a nice, long look at my ass. Heat rushed to my cheeks, yet somehow, I didn't mind. Seeing as I considered him eye candy, I guessed it was fair play for him to check me out. I couldn't resist commenting though.

"Were you just staring at my ass?"

REMY

Rachel Garrett was all kinds of trouble. She might as well have had the word tattooed on her forehead as far as I was concerned. Although, a more appropriate place for the tattoo in question would be on the swell of her breasts. Precisely where I tended to have trouble with my wandering eyes.

With her dark brown hair, flashing blue eyes, and curves for days, Rachel was downright sexy. Her sharp attitude only made her more appealing. In short, she was *my* kind of woman. This was certainly not the first time I had noticed her. I'd been living in Willow Brook for close to a year now, having moved to town after taking a position as a hotshot firefighter on a crew here.

I crossed paths with Rachel every so often through the connections of shared friends. Yet, I'd never been alone with her before. Just now, she had mud splattered on her face, all over her legs, on her arms, and smudging her shirt and shorts. All I could think was that mud wrestling with Rachel would be more than fun.

I was a gentleman though. I was also legitimately concerned she hurt herself when she almost collided with me and slipped in the mud.

"Were you just staring at my ass?" she asked.

Caught red-handed. I had, in fact, been staring at Rachel's ass. I didn't care to try to hide it and let my eyes linger just a bit longer. She had a plump, luscious bottom. With her shorts wet and molded to her body, her curves were outlined perfectly for me.

I was no misogynistic jerk. I didn't really think they were outlined for *me*, but my body sure thought so. I drank in the sight of her, my gaze coasting over the luscious curve of her ass, then to her breasts, where her nipples were visible through the fabric of her damp T-shirt and bra.

When my eyes finally reached her face, her cheeks were flushed and her eyes were flashing.

"Yes, I was," I drawled.

Despite the mud on her cheeks, I could still see her flush deepen. The air around us felt electric as Rachel stared at me. I didn't doubt for one second just how fiery Rachel would be tangled up with me.

I hadn't been interested in a woman in too damn long. I was no monk, but I could've been confused for one the last few years of my life. I shook my thoughts away from that path.

Rachel's mouth dropped open and then she snapped it shut before putting a hand on her hip and glaring at me. Little did she know that seeing her angry only sent a hot jolt of lust through me.

"Well, that was rude," she sputtered, lifting her arm and wiping the back of her hand across the mud on her cheek, an entirely pointless attempt to clean her face, especially considering her hand was covered in mud too.

A low chuckle escaped from me, and her eyes flashed again. Stepping closer, she actually wagged her finger in my face. "That's not funny."

"Darlin', you're covered in mud and you're gorgeous. I shouldn't have laughed though, so my apologies."

Yet again, her mouth opened and snapped shut.

"How's your knee?" I added.

She flexed it and shrugged. "It's fine." Then, she put her palm on my chest and gave me a little shove.

Damn, the feel of her palm against my chest was like a hot brand right through my shirt. I didn't even think, I covered her hand with mine and stepped closer. Nothing was funny now.

I wanted to kiss her. Sweet hell, did I want to kiss her. But I wouldn't. Not now. "Let's just be honest. I want you. I'll let you think on that."

At that, I released her hand and stepped back. Henry, her goofy dog, stuck his nose to the crack in the window at that moment, giving out a low woof. Rachel looked at Henry and then back at me, her blue eyes darkening. "I have to go," she said abruptly.

"You do that, sweetheart."

———

Coming March 2019!
Crash & Burn

If you love steamy, small town romance, take a visit to Diamond Creek, Alaska in my Last Frontier Lodge Series. A sexy, alpha SEAL meets his match with a brainy heroine in

Take Me Home. It's FREE on all retailers! Don't miss Gage & Marley's story!

Go here to sign up for information on new releases: http://jhcroixauthor.com/subscribe/

FIND MY BOOKS

Thank you for reading Burn For You! I hope you enjoyed the story. If so, you can help other readers find my books in a variety of ways.

1) Write a review!
2) Sign up for my newsletter, so you can receive information about upcoming new releases & receive a FREE copy of one of my books: http://jhcroixauthor.com/subscribe/
3) Like and follow my Amazon Author page at https://amazon.com/author/jhcroix
4) Follow me on Bookbub at https://www.bookbub.com/authors/j-h-croix
5) Follow me on Twitter at https://twitter.com/JHCroix
6) Like my Facebook page at https://www.facebook.com/jhcroix

Into The Fire Series
Burn For Me
Slow Burn
Burn So Bad
Hot Mess
Burn So Good
Sweet Fire
Play With Fire
Melt With You
Burn For You
Brit Boys Sports Romance
The Play
Big Win
Out Of Bounds
Play Me
Naughty Wish
Diamond Creek Alaska Novels
When Love Comes
Follow Love
Love Unbroken
Love Untamed
Tumble Into Love
Christmas Nights
Last Frontier Lodge Novels
Take Me Home
Love at Last
Just This Once
Falling Fast
Stay With Me
When We Fall
Hold Me Close
Crazy For You
Catamount Lion Shifters
Protected Mate
Chosen Mate
Fated Mate

Destined Mate
A Catamount Christmas
Ghost Cat Shifters
The Lion Within
Lion Lost & Found

ACKNOWLEDGMENTS

I will never run out of gratitude to you, my readers. Thank you (again & again & again) for cheering on my books, for your kind and funny notes, and so much more.

Many thanks to Jenn Wood for helping me make Holly & Nate's story the best it could be. Gracious thanks to Terri D. for proofreading above and beyond.

To my proofreading angels - Janine, Beth P., Terri E., Heather H., & Carolyne B. Yoly Cortez worked her magic once again, giving a new look to the entire series. I love it!

My friends and family. DBC for making me laugh and for being there no matter what. My dogs for love, joy, and sweetness.

xoxo

J.H. Croix

ABOUT THE AUTHOR

USA Today Bestselling Author J. H. Croix lives in a small town in the historical farmlands of Maine with her husband and two spoiled dogs. Croix writes steamy contemporary romance with sassy women and alpha men who aren't afraid to show some emotion. Her love for quirky small-towns and the characters that inhabit them shines through in her writing. Take a walk on the wild side of romance with her bestselling novels!

Places you can find me:
jhcroixauthor.com
jhcroix@jhcroix.com

 facebook.com/jhcroix

twitter.com/jhcroix

instagram.com/jhcroix

Printed in Great Britain
by Amazon

38125136R00138